D0366552

"That where Jimmy bunked?" he asked.

"Yeah," said Dave softly. "He got shot just outside the door."

"There'll be hell to pay."

"You got me backin' you, Horne."

"This is as far as you go, Dave. I'll go on by myself from here."

"But I . . ."

"I figure Garcia will have scouts watching his backtrail. He wants me to follow him, likely. He knows I'll come after him. Anybody else, he'll just shoot and be done with it."

"I don't know what you mean. Why won't he just shoot you?"

"He'll want me to die slow, I reckon."

Tor Books by Jory Sherman

Song of the Cheyenne
Winter of the Wolf
Horne's Law

JORY SHERMAN

HORNE'S LAW

TOR

A TOM DOHERTY ASSOCIATES BOOK
NEW YORK

All the characters and events portrayed in this book are fictitious.

HORNE'S LAW

Copyright © 1988 by Jory Sherman

All rights reserved. No part of this book may be reproduced or trans-
mitted in any form or by any means, electronic or mechanical, including
photocopying, recording, or by any information storage and retrieval
system, without permission in writing from the Publisher.

Reprinted by arrangement with Walker & Company

A Tor Book
Published by Tom Doherty Associates, Inc.
49 West 24th Street
New York, NY 10010

Cover art by Maren

ISBN: 0-812-51169-7

Library of Congress Catalog Card Number: 88-20608

First Tor edition: November 1990

Printed in the United States of America

0 9 8 7 6 5 4 3 2 1

For Alice and Dale Walker

• CHAPTER 1 •

HE STRODE THROUGH THE BLUE SHADOWS OF THAT winter morn, a tall, rawboned man whose step was careful on the narrow, winding trail just above the creek. The cold, slatecolored water burbled, whispering soft against the snow-flocked banks. The creek made its own song in the odd stillness of morning as the pale mountain jay, ghostly against the gray shroud of snowscape, marked Horne's progress along the trapline. The jay flitted from spruce to fir to pine, stirring the silence with its clawed scratch on the icy scales of trembling branches. Clumps of snow fell from each thin, sinewy limb where the bird perched, plopped with muffled thuds on the snow-covered earth.

Jackson Horne shouldered the .54 caliber Hawken caplock rifle, shifted his weight to his down-hill foot. He was a bigger man than most, standing six-foot-three in his socks, with massive broad shoulders that filled a doorframe. His face was defined by high chiseled cheekbones and a square chin, hidden under a month's growth of whiskers. His clear deep blue eyes scanned the frozen world. In the spring he would shave the beard and lean down a few pounds when he got back to breaking horses down on the flat. But his muscles were hard, finely-tuned from working the trapline, his stomach slat-smooth, the hips lean.

Each sound stretched Horne's nerves taut, amplified the ear-piercing silences in between. One minute Horne felt as if he was deaf, and the next he wondered if he should stick his fingers in his ears. If he were a mule deer he would be moving his ears independently of his head, twisting and twitching them in all directions, searching for that single isolated sound: the crunch of a man's boot on the snow, a human grunt or the rustling of clothing caught on a sapling's bare branch.

For there, along the creek bank, were the fresh tracks of a man—big-booted tracks sunk in deep. A white man's tracks, a man who had robbed the traps a week ago, before the storm, and who was now following the trapline again, picking up the marten and mink like a common thief, leaving only the blood spatters next to the sprung traps where he had knocked the animals in the head as a *coup de grace*.

Horne's mittened hand tightened on the walnut stock of his Hawken rifle as he bent to the triggered snare, examined the small stiff hairs in the braided rope. The thief had taken a rabbit from this snare, but there was no blood. This, too, gave Horne an image of the man he hunted. The hairs on the snare were from the leg—those on the ground were softer, more pliant and had come from the breast. The robber had squeezed the rabbit to death, holding its chest tight in his hand—

2

tight enough to suffocate it.

The snow was cratered where the man's knee had sunk in as he removed the kicking rabbit from the snare. Horne examined the bowl-like depression very carefully. He saw the faint claw marks where the rabbit had kicked in its last convulsions. The claw prints looked as if someone had raked a broken comb through the snow. The knee mark was smooth and Horne figured the man wore buckskins, not store-bought trousers. This was a hunch more than anything, but the concavity was without the crosshatching of woven cloth and around the edge there were small pencil-thin creases as if made by the brief drag of leather fringes.

Horne stood up, sniffed the still air, and squinted at the retreating shadows ahead. He listened intently for that one sound that did not fit into the deafening silence: the scrape of a boot on stone, the crack of a dry branch, the rattle of squaw-wood, the *whish* of snow falling from a laden spruce branch. Only the stream, curving icy through the flour-white cut that laced through the trees, sang its quiet song along rocks and rills and riffles as it wended toward the *Cache la Poudre*.

Here, in the high country above the strewn boulders of the moraines and the valleys slashed among tiered timber and rugged crags, the beaver made their dams and the deer and elk drank from trout pools. Horne no longer trapped the beaver as he once did, for it reminded him of a time best left to the past. But he valued the marten and mink, the occasional fox, and the rabbits that came to his snares and deadfalls.

These pelts still brought fair prices in Taos and Santa Fe. Horne sold the "hairy bank notes" to a buyer in Denver when he went down the mountain in the spring to see to the horses he kept wintered in Laporte, a small settlement at the foot of the mountains where the Poudre burst from the canyon onto the long plain. At least he used to, before the woman came into his home, into his life. Now, she helped dry and tan the pelts, made clothing from some of them. The full primes she saved for him to take down the mountain come spring.

A white woman with the heart and soul of a damned Arapaho. Horne gritted his teeth. Just thinking of her made something boil up in him, something he kept down lest it spill over and become something he recognized.

Yet, he wondered, why would anyone steal from such a poor trapline as his? For the money? What he earned from his five-mile line of traps over a winter season wouldn't keep a man in vittles for long. Running the trapline kept Horne from going to gut during the winter, but that was not the only reason he set traps and snares—he knew that, but had never expressed it in so many words.

It was the land, the high country, that impelled him to give up the warmth and comfort of his cabin and set his teeth to the wind, tromp through hip-high snow, plunge his bare hands into freezing water, and risk life and limb for a few prime pelts. It was breathing thin pure air that few men breathed. The air was like a drug to him, rare and precious above the timberline; he knew it was his own air, not second- or third-hand like city air that had been breathed by others.

He'd loved this place since first he stepped into the Rocky Mountains—no, even before that. When he first saw the Rockies, from far out on the plain, he felt their awesome mystery, their timeless majesty, their immense and powerful allure. He heard the French trappers talk about the peaks as if they were women, or parts of women's bodies, and

4

when he went into the mountains, he knew why they felt that way. He had grown up to manhood in the bosom of the Tetons, the enormous breasts that jutted up to the sky and made a man think of the earth as his mother. Those were powerful feelings for a young man and he had not forgotten them.

Now, he burned with anger that someone had come into his world and was trying to spoil it.

His breath blew frosty on the air and the light grew brighter, imparting a pearly cast to the snow. His sorrel gelding, Dancer, whickered from the shadows of the spruce glade where it was tied and Horne's senses jangled like Bow bells. He looked over his shoulder, saw the gelding standing rigid, Dancer's fox ears stiffened into cones, brown eyes glassy with the bounce of light.

Horne hunkered down behind a snow-flocked bush, pulled the Hawken-made rifle across his knee, flicked his thumb across the hammer's crosshatching. He listened, but heard only the incessant susurration of the stream, its monotonous murmur as it coursed past him, its dark waters glistening with liquid crystals of light.

The horse held its pose, turned its head slowly, the ear-tips twitching ever so slightly, the fine hairs aglow with eastern light. Horne felt his belly swirl, flutter as if it had been filled up with moths beating the dark air with delicate, dust-laden wings.

He heard it, then, downstream: the muffled clang of iron on stone. The creek took a bend below him and he could not see beyond, but his mind pinpointed the location. There was another trap down there, set close by the brook on an icy slide, where the mink fished for red-speckled trout that swarmed in the deep pool gouged out by years of rushing spring waters.

He could see the place in his mind, see it clear.

The snow was frozen there, watered down by the minks using it as a launching pad. He had set the trap in the water, stunk it up good. Straddling the frozen slide were small fir trees and above that, on a knoll, was a well-worn game trail through a thick stand of spruce, rocks and brush. Horne would have to be careful approaching the trap area. He looked up the slope, past the gelding. The game trail was up there, but the snow was deeper. The ridge humped out there, above the mink slide. He looked at the snowshoes dangling from his saddle horn. Once up on the trail, he would need them, but they could be treacherous. And, they made noise. No, he would not use the snowshoes.

Horne stood up, heard again the clink of metal against a rock. Something about it did not sound quite right. He couldn't put a thumb on what was wrong, but the oddness of the sound struck him and stayed clogged in his mind. He shook off the feeling, grabbed the forestock of the Hawken for balance and took the slope on an angle. He trudged into the deeper snow, his moccasin soles sliding on the slick underfooting.

He had an eerie feeling about that sound. Something about it rang warning klaxons in his mind. He heard the trap bang against stone again and wondered what was making the noise. A man? An animal? The latter, perhaps. It was a noise that should have sounded once, maybe twice, and then faded away. But, it seemed to come at regular intervals and it did not seem like the kind of sound a wounded animal might make. There was no urgency to it, no change in pitch or loudness. No in-between sounds. That's what bothered him most. Just that sound, no other. No scuffle, no ring of trap chain. Only the clatter of a trap on a rock, always sounding the same.

Horne gained the narrow game trail, probably

made long ago by sheep brought to the high country in summer by Basques who had since moved on to the flat grasslands not claimed by cattle or sodbusters. He sloughed through the drifts, heard his boot moccasins hiss as though he waded through a thick field of tall bluestem. His footwear was beaded and waterproofed with tallow, his feet dry. His buckskins, too, were dry and he wore a four-point capote made from a Hudson Bay trade blanket—all wool and warm as a fire when he pulled the hood up over his head. He had the hood down, now, listening for sounds other than the clanking iron, but he heard only the whisper of the snow against his leggings and the low, sizzling hiss of his soles sliding with every step. He had to guard against skidding off the game trail. Despite its thickness, the snow was slick underneath the thin crust on top, thawed and refrozen during sun-filled days and bone-chilling nights.

The bleak sun softened the shadows, glinted off the snow and the creek waters. Horne squinted. A man could go temporarily blind in the midday glare of such light. The whiteness of the land was magnified as the sun rose, fought to shine through the gray batting of clouds—sugar white, as if he had stumbled into an enormous sugar bin. He looked away from the monotonous white creek toward the dark trunks of the trees. Even so, he almost missed seeing it.

Above the place where he had set the trap, he saw some string. It was made from leather thongs tied together and one end was tied to a bare tree that had been killed by lightning. As Horne jerked it, he heard the clank of the trap, saw it drop from a small spruce and strike a stone on the bank of the stream. Horne dove for the ground just as the rifle boomed thirty yards above him. He saw the orange flash, the puff of white smoke, just before the ball struck him high on the head, knocking his beaver hat into a tree. He saw lights dance in his head and darkness enveloped him as he ploughed headlong into the snow, leaving a streak of red in the pristine whiteness of a wind-blown mound. Somewhere in the darkness he heard another shot, but it sounded far away, almost like someone snapping his fingers in a dark, empty room.

Then, the echo of the shot faded as the darkness closed over him, wrapping him in a shroud that blotted out all sound and feeling.

• CHAPTER 2 •

JULES MOREAUX HEARD THE GUNSHOT, THE HEAVY roll of thunder from a big caliber weapon. The sound reverberated through the canyon as he looked up toward the ridge. He stood on the bank of the Poudre, a fishing line in his hand. He had three trout in a woven willow creel bobbing at water's edge. He had no pole, only bare gut line with an antelope bone hook and a red swatch of cloth just back of the sharpened point.

He heard another shot and tried to pinpoint its origin. He scanned the high slopes, but the white smoke, if any, was invisible against the glare of snow. He heard a distant noise, the snap of a branch, then a spellbinding silence that gripped him, froze him into immobility for several seconds. It was a mountain silence, deep and awesome, puzzling in its loudness. Jules felt his heart sink as if weighted with lead. His belly swirled and fluttered like leaves in a windstorm. He

9

dropped the line into the eddying pool of water, reached for his Hawken rifle. This was trouble, he knew, without being told. Jackson Horne ran his trapline up on that tree-stippled slope and if there was trouble it wasn't just for Horne, but for all of them in Sky Valley. Trouble that had been brewing ever since Horne had gone after the Arapaho and rescued one of the three sisters kidnapped by Red Hawk's men. It had taken a year to do it, but Horne found them. He killed Red Hawk and brought back Mary Lee Simmons, the only girl who had survived.

Jules, and everyone else in the valley, knew damned well where Horne's trapline lay: west of the Poudre and north of the creek. That was Horne's territory, though he may not have claimed it on paper, and it was little enough in such a big land as this.

He stepped back from the stream, wary. He checked the cap on his gun nipple, pressed it down out of habit. The rifle was armed. Jules started toward his horse tied in the willows below him. His features darkened in a scowl as he sniffed the faint aroma of acrid burnt powder drifting to him on the light breeze of morning. He was what some people called a *breed*. His father was French, killed by his mother's people for bedding another man's wife against her will. His mother was Lakota, of the Unkpapa tribe. After his father was killed, Jules had run away from the lodge and had taken up with the free trappers. He married a Santa Fe woman, Maria Montes, and settled down in Sky Valley some time after Horne had come there. He had known Horne during the trapping days, but they had never been friends, nor were they now. But Jules respected the man, feared him more than a little.

He slipped into the willows, untied his horse, a

10

stocky paint that he had bought from Horne after the business with the Arapaho. He led the animal out of the thicket and mounted him. The Santa Fe saddle creaked under his weight, settled against the horse's back, snug with the single cinch.

There was a ford upstream from him and he rode there, letting the Indian pony pick its way over the slick bare rocks, the mounds of snow. He crossed the narrows, kept to cover as he criss-crossed up the opposite slope. He heard another shot that made his blood quicken, and then the graveyard stillness returned. He waited for another shot, but none came. Instead, he heard the beat of a horse's hoofs high above him that faded into another silence, a silence that was even deeper than before.

Jules's eyes were black as coal chunks as he scanned the slope above him. He saw the bright splash of a green capote through a break in the fir and spruce trees. It was not moving. Jules recognized the garment. It belonged to Horne. The breed rode toward it, his finger inside the trigger guard of the Hawken, his thumb on the hammer. The pony floundered through deep drifts and heaved from the exertion and altitude.

Jules guided the paint up the slope, crisscrossing in a switchback pattern to keep from tiring the pony and to keep it on a level footing as much as was possible on the slippery snow beneath the thin crust. He gave the animal its head on the side-hill, only reined it when he wanted it to change direction. The horse kicked up clumps of snow as it fought for footing on the steep slope, its muscles bunching whenever it shifted its course.

He reached the place where Horne had fallen, drew in a breath when he saw the flecks of blood—stark crimson against the pure whiteness of the snow.

11

Horne lay against a rock, his eyes closed. Blood smeared the snow under his shoulder. Jules looked around, saw the leather string, the trap attached to it. Below, the mink slide glistened like mica-infested stone shot with the glinting rays of the morning sun. He couldn't put it together yet, but Horne was either hurt bad or dead.

"Horne?"

There was no answer.

Jules dismounted, tied the rope reins to a juniper. He clambered toward the fallen man, knelt by his side. He leaned down over the man, felt Horne's hot breath blow faintly on his cheek. He touched Horne's forehead.

"Horne, can you hear me? It is Jules Moreaux, eh? I come to help you. You wake up now, Horne, pretty quick, eh?"

He felt behind Horne's head for the lump he knew must be there. The man had struck the rock, apparently, and was unconscious from that. Jules could see the place where Horne's body had skidded down to the rock. The blood on the snow was not from the blow to the head. Moreaux rocked back on his bent legs and pulled Horne toward him, saw the ragged tear in the wounded man's capote. Gingerly, he felt the wound. Blood pumped onto his fingers and he knew this was not a good sign. There was a lot of blood and it was still flowing.

Horne winced with the touch and his eyes batted open. He looked into Jules's face with a glazed look in his eyes.

"Horne? You are hurt pretty bad, I think."

"Moreaux. Ah." Horne grunted, sucked in a breath. "Somebody tried to slam the coffin lid down on me."

"I think maybe you mighty lucky, Horne. Maybe somebody want to kill you, eh?"

Horne struggled to sit up on his own.

Jules's face blurred before him. Pain shot through his left wrist, below where the shoulder wound pumped blood. There was more blood below. He felt a lump. Moreaux watched as Horne pulled back the loose sleeve of his capote. There, buried in the wrist, was the ball. Horne plucked it out of his flesh and the wound gushed freshets of blood. Pump, pump, pump and he felt the lassitude of weakness wash over him. His ears buzzed and rang with an empty, hollow, far-off roar, like the keening in a seashell.

Horne grabbed his wrist with his right hand, squeezed it hard to shut off the blood.

He looked at Jules cockeyed, then toppled over on his side.

Moreaux swore.

Horne's hand relaxed and the blood spurted from the ragged, bluish hole in his wrist.

"Ay de mi!" Jules cried out. He drew his long-bladed knife, one seasoned in a Santa Fe smithy's ironwood fire, and cut the sleeve away from Horne's arm, slashed a strip of green wool from it. Quickly, he lashed the makeshift tourniquet to Horne's arm, just below the elbow, tied a loose knot. He groped in the snow for a stick, found a frozen branch and slipped it through the knot. He twisted the stick in a circle, tightening the tourniquet until the blood stopped pumping through the wound.

Jules knew he wouldn't have much time. The wound must be tended, the tourniquet loosened at intervals. If not, then Horne might lose his arm. Might even die. There was so much blood, Jules guessed the ball must have opened up an artery.

Jules got up and brought his pony over to the wounded man. He struggled to lift the big man from the snow. Horne was a dead weight. Jules slid his hands under the hurt man's armpits, tugged hard. Grunting, he pulled Horne to his knees. He would never get the man across the paint's back this way.

He laid Horne back down onto the snow, swung the pony around so that he stood below, on the low side of the slope. He jerked the reins in hard, tapped the paint on its knees. The horse buckled, came down to a kneeling position. Jules straddled the animal, reached over the saddle and grabbed Horne's capote with both hands. He bunched the wool up in his hands just below Horne's neck, jerked the man toward the horse. He managed to heft Horne's torso up onto the saddle and pull him across the seat. Then, he prodded the pony back to its feet.

After taking a hemp rose from his saddle kit, Jules lashed the wounded hunter to the horse, crisscrossing the rope into a modified diamond hitch. He picked up Horne's Hawken, wiped most of the snow from its barrel and stock, carried it in his left hand. Then, he led his paint upslope toward Horne's own horse. He walked alongside, made sure Horne did not slip from the saddle. The going was slow and Horne rocked back and forth with every step the paint took up the uneven slope.

Jules knew that Horne might die. Even with the tourniquet, Horne might bleed to death if the artery in his wrist had been opened up.

The breed floundered in a half-circle until he gained footing on the trail broken that morning by Horne. Pulling the pony and its human cargo behind him, Jules followed the track until he came to Horne's horse. The sorrel gelding, a one-man horse, shied and jerked at its reins as Jules drew near. He calmed the horse, spoke to it in soothing tones as he shook the reins free of the spruce branch. He sheathed the Hawken in the buffalo-hide boot he knew that Horne had made. It rode just in front of the right stirrup, attached to the saddle with thick thongs. He loosened the tourniquet around Horne's arm, then tightened it again when the blood began to gush through the bullet hole.

"Horne," said Moreaux. "You in a pretty bad way, I think."

The big man moaned but made no reply. Jules mounted the wounded man's horse, pulled his pony up alongside. Slowly, he picked his way along the backtrail, heading for Horne's cabin deep in the woods of Sky Valley. He hadn't seen the Simmons girl since that day Horne brought her back to the valley after tracking her kidnappers, but he'd heard that she was living with Horne. Her parents, Louis and Elizabeth Simmons, had been grief-stricken over the deaths of their two daughters who had been ravaged and killed by the Indians before Horne caught Red Hawk and the others. But instead of being grateful to Horne, the parents hated him for bringing back the sullied Mary Lee. Later, they hated her for taking up with him instead of returning to their home.

There had been a lot of talk about that in the valley, especially among the newcomers who had been moving in and bringing more of civilization with them. Some accused Horne of taking advantage of Mary Lee, both on the long ride back from the Platte River, and since. Some men grew angry just knowing that there was a young unmarried woman living in Horne's cabin with him, living in sin.

The man who was most vocal about the situation was Dan Reinhardt, who seemed to take a personal interest in Horne. Reinhardt had befriended Lou Simmons, had listened to his tale of

Horne and his daughters. He had listened to Bill McPherson, as well, a man who hated Horne as much as anyone, although he could give no good reason why. Horne had been disliked ever since the early settlers moved into the valley, long after Horne had built his cabin. People had resented the lone man who lived on the edge of their small civilization. Now as the stories about Mary Lee and Horne grew and stretched into lies, most of the settlers seemed to hate him even more than before. Never mind that they had begged Horne to help them after the Arapahoes had killed Caleb McGonigle and little Angus McPherson before abducting the Simmons girls. He had agreed to go after the Arapahoes but only if he could do it *his* way, alone.

Jules guessed that Bill McPherson and the others hated Horne because Horne held them all in contempt, would not mingle with them or join in small talk at McGonigle's when the men sat around the pot-bellied stove and solved all the world's problems.

Jules Moreaux tried to stay out of it, but he had ears to hear with and when the men gathered at McGonigle's Trading Post (they still called it that, even though Caleb was dead), he heard them speak against Horne as if he was the enemy of progress, the boulder in the path of community growth. Horne had been hated before he went after the girls, but he was hated even more after his return. The same men who had asked Horne for his help now seemed ashamed that they had gone to Horne; in fact, some of them denied it, saying Horne had taken it upon himself to go after the Arapaho.

Mary Lee's father was the most bitter of all. Old Louis Simmons spoke most loudly against Horne. He had been struck hard on the head by the marauding Indians and some said he had not been quite right since. He had turned to brooding, but more dangerously, it was he who kept the stories alive, he who told the biggest lies about Horne and poisoned the newcomers' minds against a man most of them had never seen close up.

Jules wondered about Mary Lee, though. He knew her mother pined for her and asked Louis time and again to go and fetch her from Horne. But Louis never would go and he said he never wanted to see his daughter again. Elizabeth Simmons had gone to see her once, Jules knew, but her daughter had slammed the door in her face, breaking her heart once again.

He rode on through the widening morning, the sun sending light shafts through the trees, sparkling off the snow. The horses' hoofs made muffled sounds as they broke through the thickening crust. He smelled woodsmoke from Horne's cabin long before he reached it and he knew the girl would be home. He wondered what he would say to her and if she would want him to fetch help for her man.

He wondered, too, what would happen to her if Horne should die. She would be left all alone.

•CHAPTER 3•

JULES ADJUSTED THE TOURNIQUET OFTEN DURING THE
two hours it took to ride to Horne's place.
Dried blood encrusted both wounds and the
artery seemed not to be pumping so much the last
few times he loosened the stick of wood that
served as a tourniquet. But Horne was very pale
and was still unconscious. There was a brown
streak across the side of his forehead. It looked
as if someone had laid a hot poker against the flesh
for just a brief moment. His face was cold and
clammy, so were his mittened hands.

A horse whinnied as Jules rode up to the cabin.
Dancer whickered in reply, his rubbery nostrils
quivering as they shot out jets of steam. The door
to the cabin opened and Jules saw the faint outline of the woman standing there in shadow. He
called out when he saw the rifle barrel jutting
through the doorway, its black snout pointing
straight at him.

"Hello the house!"

"What have you got there?" called out Mary Lee. "What are you doing on that horse?"

"It is Horne. He is hurt pretty bad, I think."

"Horne!" she squealed. He saw the rifle barrel drop and heard the hardwood butt strike the floor.

She flew toward him across the snow and he saw she was wearing a buckskin dress, her red hair tied in twin braids, bright ribbons intertwined in the russet strands. She wore the moccasin boots, too, and she looked, Jules thought, more Indian than white as she raced toward him, fleet as a deer. He reined up Dancer and the pony stopped, shivered and shook under its burden as if to dislodge Horne and be free of the weight.

"What have you done to him?" Mary Lee shrieked as she saw Horne's body draped across the Santa Fe saddle, tied there like a game animal. She began tugging at the hitch knot and uttering low sounds in her throat.

"I did nothing to him, Mary Lee," said Jules. "I found him shot, lying in the snow. Be careful you do not make him bleed more."

She turned, focused her eyes upward at Jules, a look of helplessness and bewilderment flickering in her eyes. But her expression quickly hardened and there was a glint of determination in her eye.

Jules noticed that tiny freckles still mottled her face, looking like cinnamon sprinkled on her cheeks. Her copper hair had turned a dark russet, and she had filled out from the girl he had last seen. Her smoky hazel eyes flashed defiance, but her pursed lips trembled slightly as if she might break into tears at any time. The buckskin dress clung to her figure and the leggings could not hide the trimness of her legs and ankles. She wore an Arapaho love bracelet on her wrist and when she saw Jules looking at it, she slid it up her arm, hid it under her sleeve. Her bosom pressed against the buckskin yoke of her dress, pushed the laces taut across her wide, comely chest. Her tummy strained under the buckskin garment, a little roundness that was barely noticeable.

Yes, thought Jules, she had grown into a woman.

"We get him inside," he said softly. "I think he has lost much blood."

"Wha—what happened?" she asked.

"Some man shot this one, I think. He run off when I come up from the river. The ball hit the shoulder, come out the wrist, eh? There is one big vein under those little bones. The artery, maybe. Still bleeds pretty good, eh?"

"Yes," she said breathlessly, "I will take care of Horne." There was iron in her voice and Jules's eyebrows arched. He began untying the hitch knot.

"Make him a place inside the cabin," said Moreaux. "I will carry him."

"Yes," said Mary Lee tightly and she ran to the cabin, opened the door wide. Jules slid Horne from the pony's back, carried the man like an oversized child to the cabin. His bandy legs bowed under the weight of this man he had once trapped with in the brigades, but had never known well.

None of the mountain men had known Horne very well. He was one of those who always stood apart, although he always did his share and more besides. Horne kept to himself even when he walked beside a man.

Jules staggered into the murky interior of the cabin. Firelight danced from the hearth, hurled shadows against the log walls; it striped the floor and made the beamed ceiling teeter and glow, shrink and expand, billow and suck up like a breathing thing. Mary Lee beckoned to him from across the room and he saw the bed she had turned down for Horne. It was solidly made from handhewn logs, trimmed with an axe, stood at one end of the cabin. A bedroll, rumpled from someone sleeping in it, lay atop a bearskin rug in front of the stone fireplace and Jules knew without asking that this was where the woman slept.

The blazing logs threw orange light on the rug, made it glisten and shine copper against the deep black of its pile. The hide pulsed like something alive and bristled with the rippling sheen of the flames blowing through its dark hairs like vagrant sunlight stirring a tawny prairie wind. Jules thought of softness and warmth and wondered how a man like Horne could let a woman sleep alone like that, warmed only by the fire and the deep fur of the bear's hide. It was a thing he did not understand, but he knew there was much about Horne that was puzzling.

He laid the wounded man gently on the big bed, knelt beside him to loosen the tourniquet once again.

"You see, eh?" he said. "Too dam' tight, too much tight. You make loose, then make tight, eh? Ever' five minute."

"Yes. I know what to do."

"Maybe he needs sewing up, eh? Or, you put a hot iron on the wounds to seal them up."

Blood trickled through the wound now that the tourniquet was loosened. Mary Lee knelt beside Jules, touched a finger to the wound in Horne's wrist. Blood pooled up on her fingertip and she lifted it to her mouth, tasted it. She leaned over, kissed the wound and there was blood on her lips.

"You want Jules to bring help?" he asked.

"No," she said sharply, "you must not tell anyone Horne is hurt. Do you understand?"

"Yes, but this man . . . he hurt bad. Maybe bleed to death."

"No he won't!" she said. "I will fix his wounds." She touched the blue-black place on his shoulder,

21

winced as if she could feel the pain that Horne, in his cocoon of sleep, could not.

"I will send my woman," said Jules, rising to his feet.

"No," she said again. "I—I'll not need her."

"I go now," said Jules.

"Wait," she said, standing up. "Who did this? Who shot Horne?"

He felt her eyes—greenish brown, flecked with gold, and darkening—as she pierced him with her stare, locked on his, and he knew he could not turn away from her or she would probably attack him.

"I do not know," he said evenly, but his gaze faltered under her withering stare.

"You do not know? Or will not tell me?" Her mocking tone lanced him, nicked his pride.

"I truly do not know," he said, and that was the truth.

"But you—you"—she groped for the word—"suspect someone."

"No," he said.

"Jules, someone was robbing Horne's traps, his snares. A week ago. Maybe he found out who it was. Did you see anyone? Did you see tracks? Please. Horne will want to know. I want to know."

Yes, he knew Horne would want to know. Horne, if he lived, would kill the man who wounded him. He would do it quick and without much talk. That was the way Horne was. Jules shuddered to think about it. He remembered the day Horne returned with the girl and Luke Newcastle tried to shoot Horne. Horne would have let the man live, let him take whatever punishment the townsfolk would have meted out to him, but Newcastle drew his pistol and Horne shot him dead and walked away without a word. People still talked about that, and they said Horne killed in cold blood, but he had not. He had been deliberate and cool, but his was an act of self-defense. If he had not killed Newcastle, Luke would have killed him.

"There were tracks."

"Do you know who made them?"

"No. I did not look hard. Horne, he was hurt. Blood, eh? I go back, follow the tracks, maybe."

"Yes, Jules. Find out who shot Horne. Please."

"I go," he said. "I put away Horne's horse and go back to that place, eh?"

"Yes," she said. "Find out who shot Horne."

Jules looked again at the cabin before he left. No one had ever been inside before. It was a man's place, but he saw traces of the woman, too. Traps and cooking irons were things he had in his own home, pots and pans, as well. But there were pillows and doilies made from ermine and otter, tanned hides decorated with berry juice and beads and porcupine quills. He smelled venison stew simmering on the iron cookstove and the odor of onions and turnips that made his mouth water. She did not show much, some young women did not, but Jules guessed that she was with child. Her cheeks glowed and her breasts were full. Weeks along maybe? Was it Horne's child? He wondered.

"You don't tell anyone, Jules, hear?" Mary Lee called to him as he reached the door. He turned, saw her stripping the capote from Horne's torso gently, sliding it off his huge frame as though she were unpacking bone china. He mumbled assent and went back outside into the cold, the heat suddenly shut off and his breath spewing smoke. He led the tall gelding around the cabin to the corral and stables, stripped it of saddle and traps, put grain in a bin, saw to it that the water trough was not frozen. Chunks of ice floated in it showing Horne had broken the lid up that morning and it

23

had not refrozen. He walked back to his own pony, climbed wearily into the saddle.

He rode back in the direction from which he had come, sad because he knew he could follow those tracks with his eyes shut. He knew who had made them, but there wasn't a damned thing he could do about it.

Mary Lee Simmons gently removed Horne's undergarments, looked at his scarred body. She touched a slash across his chest, fought back the tears. He looked so big and helpless lying there, his shoulder caked with dried blood, his wrist throbbing under the tourniquet. She bit her lip and turned away.

Mary Lee picked up the .45 caliber mountain rifle and leaned it next to the door. She set the latch and dropped the bolt on the door of the cabin, put more wood on the hearth. She emptied a wooden bucket of water she had filled from the creek into an iron pot and put it on the woodstove. She put more faggots in the firebox, stirred the coals vigorously with a stick of kindling. Horne moaned and she went to him quickly. She touched his forehead. It was cool and clammy, so oddly lifeless she cringed inside.

"Oh, Horne," she breathed.

She looked at the scars and wrinkles on his chest and stomach before bracing herself to check the wound on his shoulder. She had seen those scars before, wondered about them. She knew a lot about Horne, the way he was now, knew his moods and his ways, but she knew very little of his past. He had not seen her looking at him because she had done it in secret, as she did so many things under his roof when he was inside.

It frightened her now to think that Horne might die. She felt the flutter of moths in her stomach,

the nervous contractions of fear that made her
quiver inside, made her hands start to tremble.
She thought of the long lone days with Horne
when he was bringing her back to the valley, how
he had saved her from the wild cougars, protected
her at risk to his own life. Yet he had never asked
for anything in return.

She knew everyone in Sky Valley saw her ride
home with Jackson Horne after he brought her
back. She was the only survivor of the Arapaho
kidnapping. Her two sisters had been murdered
by Red Hawk, scalped. Horne brought their scalps
back, gave them to her father. Everyone expected
Mary Lee to go back to her family, to run to her
mother's arms and embrace her father. But she
didn't go back. The girl, they said afterward, just
took up with Horne shamelessly and most folks,
she knew, figured the whole ordeal had addled her
mind like it had her father's. "No sane woman
would keep house for such a man as Horne," said
Luke's widow, Charity Newcastle, one day when
Mary Lee was at McGonigle's—said it loud enough
so that Mary Lee could hear.

What none of them knew was that Horne hadn't
invited Mary Lee to stay with him. He didn't boot
her out of his cabin, however. She just took up
with him gradual-like and began cooking his
meals, cleaning up the cabin, mending his clothes,
washing them. When he worked the hides, she'd
come up beside him, pick up a tool and begin to
help him. She felt a strong bond between them,
but it was unrequited and pained her so to think
of it.

"You don't give me much," she said to him one
day.

"I said you could stay until you got your mind
settled some," he replied. "You got folks, a place
to stay."

25

"I want to stay with you, Horne," she said quietly.

"You got to make peace with your folks, Mary Lee."

She had clouded over like a winter sky, she remembered, bowed her head and felt as if no one would ever know what was in her heart. No one. It was hard going back to the life you left when things had changed for you. After living with the Arapaho for a year or so, she had things churning around inside her brain that had to be set right. She was sure Horne understood some of her feelings. Sometimes he would look at her long and hard and she could almost hear the speech forming in his throat, the words gathering like storm clouds over the high rocky crags above the valley. But he would just growl and the words fell apart or he swallowed them into that massive scarred chest of his and walked away, leaving her to shake like a thin young aspen in autumn. She longed for him to take her in his arms and hold her tight against him until she stopped quivering—until the things inside her flowed into him and what he had in his heart flowed into her. Then there would be no need for speech to express these sad, tangled-up feelings she'd had ever since that brutal, bloody day when Red Hawk invaded her life.

"Horne," she said bitterly one day, when he told her once again she ought to go back home to her folks, "you don't know a damned thing."

"I know you got feelings," he said simply and she wanted to run to him then and burn his face with her kisses, swarm over him like a cloud of wild bees on a honeycomb. Instead, she had wiped away unbidden tears and looked into the distance, into a mist of mountains that had no shape or form but were like a giant wall closing her in and keeping her out at the same time.

But she knew Horne understood some of her

feelings. He had shown her that on the trail back to the valley, giving her silence when she needed it, talking to her when she wanted to hear a human voice speaking in English. He knew of her unspoken grief over her dead sisters, the horror of knowing they had been scalped and thrown away like old, tattered dolls with the stuffing ripped out of them. He knew that she had formed some kind of strange attachment to Red Hawk, her kidnapper, her cruel captor.

Oh, yes, Horne knew she had the bad dreams and that she sometimes drifted away, her spirit, her hidden self; and that she got a faraway look in her eyes and couldn't see things up close, couldn't face him knowing that he knew about her—what Red Hawk had done to her and what she had done with him in his lodge. Somehow, she didn't mind Horne knowing, because he had known Red Hawk long before she had, had loved a woman that Red Hawk had thrown away after taking her from Horne. She didn't want to be thrown away like that, by Horne or by her folks. That's what she wanted to tell him, but never could. Not until now, when he could not hear her.

"I just can't go back home," she said to him now. "Horne, are you listening? I can't go back home. Ever."

Horne lay there on the bed, floating deep under waves of sleep like a man dead on a slow-moving river.

"It ain't easy going back home to folks who would always look at me oddly, knowin' I shared Red Hawk's blanket and was violated by those same murderin' braves who killed Caleb McGonigle and little Angus McPherson.

"They would never understand," she added, her voice faded to a quiet that made the room seem small and dark, and made her feel all alone.

•CHAPTER 4•

MARY LEE FELT CAREFULLY AROUND HORNE'S shoulder wound, pushed her finger inside the small hole, feeling for splinters of bone. She breathed a sigh of relief when she felt no protrusions. She felt down his arm and loosened the tourniquet once again, probed the exit hole in his wrist one more time. Horne's breathing quickened, but he did not awaken. There were no broken bones in the wrist, but the blood continued to leak through the ragged flesh surrounding the hole. She let out a sigh of relief that she would not have to probe for the lead ball.

Once, when she was a captive of Red Hawk's band, one of the braves, a man named Gray Deer, had brought in a wounded warrior. The Arapaho had been shot with a .44 caliber pistol at close range. There were flecks of unexploded black powder embedded in the man's flesh around the wound. He was struck in the shoulder and the ball had entered the bone. Owl Lady cleaned the man's wound and then crawled aside in the lodge as Red Hawk and Gray Deer squatted over the wounded man, Big Wolf, each with a pair of brass bullet molds in his hands. Mary Lee's sisters did not want to watch the primitive surgery, but Mary Lee had stayed, fascinated by the procedure.

Gray Deer wiped the wound with a piece of buckskin, then plunged his bullet mold inside. Red Hawk opened the mouth of his mold and inserted it on the other side of the bone where the bullet was lodged. They could not get a good grip on the flattened ball with the tong-like molds, but they persisted. Bleeding made the ball slippery and the sharp edges of the molds kept sliding off the lead. Finally, Red Hawk asked Owl Lady and Mary Lee, whom he called Sun Hair, to hold Big Wolf down. He and Gray Deer gave strong tugs on the bullet molds, but they broke loose, tearing out small chunks of the soft lead. Red Hawk grunted and drew his knife, ordering the others to hold the brave down even harder than before. Big Wolf never made a sound while all this was happening and Mary Lee marveled at his stoical calm. Red Hawk ran his sharp-bladed knife down into the collar bone close to the lead ball. He worked the knife from side to side to loosen the wedged ball. At last, he gave a grunt of satisfaction and flipped the ball out of the bone. He grabbed it and held it up for all to see. Gray Deer smiled. Big Wolf grinned too, and throughout the ordeal, she remembered, he never so much as flinched.

After that, Mary Lee asked Owl Lady a lot of questions about Arapaho medicine and she learned which herbs took away pain, which could heal sores and wounds, and those, like the sweet pine with fungus, which, when smoked, could purify the body. She knew that none of these things would help Horne. But, she knew that somehow she had to stop the bleeding. On closer examination, she saw that the ball had exited above the wrist. Blood had flowed down to the wrist and coagulated, making it look like one large wound.

When the water was boiling, she cut up thin sackcloth and dipped it in the kettle. She swabbed the wound, cleaned off the dried blood. She washed a fire tong, placed it in the fireplace over the flames. When the tip was cherry red, she wrapped the handle in damp cloth to give her a better grip, carried it to Horne's side. She had seen cauterization done one day at McGonigle's, when Chollie Winder had put a hot knife to his son Gary's leg in order to seal off a wound the boy had got when he ran a pitchfork through his calf.

Now, she held Horne's arm down flat and gently dropped the red-hot tip of the tong onto the wound. The hissing sound of burning flesh broke the silence; the smell of burnt skin wafted to her nostrils. She fought off a queasiness that roiled her stomach. She withdrew the tong, saw pieces of skin writhe as they burned on the iron. She looked at Horne's wound, saw that the flesh was fused together, the blackened skin forming a crust. She winced, loosened the tourniquet.

The bleeding had stopped.

Horne stirred, opened his eyes. Tears brimmed the ducts, flowed down his face. Mary Lee saw the pain there, like a murky shadow in a stream. To her surprise, Horne grinned weakly.

"You do it right, girl?" he asked.

She nodded dumbly.

"Obliged," he croaked and his eyes closed again. She felt his arm relax, then quiver for several seconds. But, Horne did not bleed from the wrist wound anymore. Quickly, she began to tend to the entrance hole in Horne's shoulder. She searched among her few things for the sewing basket she had woven from bullrushes.

She found a needle stuck in a pin cushion she had made from a scrap of cloth and a small pine cone. She looked in her sewing kit for an awl that would suit her purpose. She had kept several from her days with Red Hawk. She chose one made from the spine taken from a large catfish. It was strong and sharp-pointed, much better than the tough thorn awl or those fashioned from antelope bone sharpened to a fine point. She also had an awl that was ground down from a worn out knife blade, but this was much too big to use on Horne's wound. The needle was curved, sharp, made from a small rib-bone of a trout. She had sinew, but thought she might use the twisted bark of the milkweed that she had saved. In time, she knew, the milkweed would dissolve, or she could remove it once the wound had healed.

She set to work, puncturing the skin with the awl, then sewing the wound shut. Later, she wiped the sweat and tears from Horne's face, sat beside him as he slept, wondering if the salve he used to doctor his horses would work on his wounds.

Jules Moreaux cursed himself for having come to Horne's aid. He thought of the fish still in the creel and his wife at home wondering why he had not slept well and had wanted to leave again. And, where were the fish? She had asked him that and he had lied to her, told her that he had left them there in the Poudre when a bear had run him off. But, she knew this was not a time for bears. Not this high up. Not in Sky Valley in late January. There had been no need to go back to the place where Horne was shot yesterday. He knew where the tracks of the bushwhacker would lead. He knew the name of the man who had shot Horne. It was a stupid thing to do.

He rode the paint through the snow-choked woods, heading in the direction of the man's cabin, wishing he had gone straight over there the day before. But, he had not wanted to see the man when perhaps his blood was running hot and his temper aflare. Now, when he had had time to cool, maybe the man would listen to reason. Maybe he would pack up and leave the valley before Horne recovered from his wounds. Jules almost laughed aloud. Dan Reinhardt did not strike him as a man who would move like that. He was like a boulder in the trail, if he read him right. Like Horne, in some ways, but meaner, something bad boiling in him, a strong hate that he brought to the valley from somewhere. And Simmons had been feeding his ear, telling him things about Horne and Mary Lee. Reinhardt was a single man, looking for a wife, and that was no good in this valley. There were no single women now that the other Simmons girls had been murdered. There was just Mary Lee and she was Horne's woman.

Jules knew very little about Reinhardt. He had come up to Sky Valley from the flatland, El Pueblo, before that, Santa Fe. He had brought trade goods, sold them to Kurt Jaeger, who had taken over McGonigle's. Jules gathered that Kurt and Dan had known each other before. They were both Germans and Kurt had been to Santa Fe more than once since settling in the valley.

Secrets. The valley was full of secrets, especially now. More newcomers had come after Reinhardt, and like him, they had knocked down trees and built cabins, staking out portions of the land for themselves. Lou Simmons encouraged settlers to come and when they did, he told them his sad story and drew their sympathies. He filled them with hatred for the man he hated—Horne.

Jules wanted to defend Horne, but every time he opened his mouth to say something, he was beaten back with angry words from a dozen men. Finally, he had just kept his mouth shut and let them all talk, say what they wanted to say about Horne and the Simmons girl. But, it made him sick and now he was sick again. Mary Lee had told him not to say anything about Horne, but Reinhardt had to know. The German would tell the others, no doubt. And maybe they would go at Horne like wolves, try to finish him off when he was down.

Jules thought of his wife, Maria, the Santa Fe woman who was not able to bear him children. She did not know of any of these things. She did not feel comfortable around the other women and seldom spoke when she went with Jules to Mc-Gonigle's. She spoke only a little English, no French. She and Jules conversed in Spanish, which had come to seem almost as natural to him as his native French. She knew about Horne because Jules had spoken of him often, but she did not like to be reminded of Jules's past, when he was a free trapper with Horne and the other wild men of the mountains. She listened when he wanted to talk, but never encouraged him to speak of the past by bringing it up herself. She was satisfied with him the way he was now. They had plans to buy cattle and start their own ranch. She saved cash like some people stored fruit and vegetable preserves and spoke of the place they would have someday, perhaps further south where the Rio Grande was born or along the Arkansas.

Jules earned cash money by hunting and trapping, running cattle as a drover during the summer. Maria made clothing from her loom and pot-

tery that she sold in Denver. Whatever they didn't
need for survival, she hoarded, keeping the money
hidden even from Jules, the amount written in a
ledger she kept locked up in her trunk. Jules never
asked her how much money they had. He trusted
her as he trusted no man, and he was content to
live free and look to the future, even though he
regretted that Maria was not able to bear children.

At the last rendezvous on the Siskeedee Agie,
what some called the Green River, word had come
that the Government of the U.S. had offered emigrants 640 acres of land and Jules had begun to
think it was time to take him a wife and get out
of the mountains. Horne had already left and
when Bob Newell said he was going to sell his furs
at Fort Hall, Jules had gone with him. Some of
the mountain men had taken to stealing, something that had never been done before, and Jules,
like Newell, was disgusted when ten or fifteen men
left camp to go to California and steal horses.
Newell had come to rendezvous with Drips, Fraeb,
and Bridger from St. Louis, and when they ran
into Clark Smith Littlejohn and some Mormon
missionaries, Clark told them about the free land.
The rendezvous was wild, with Horne killing a
man who had kidnapped some Indian girls and
then Moses Harris trying to kill Bob Newell with
an eighty-yard shot.

Newell wasn't hurt, but he was mad. It seemed
time to give up the life of trapping and when Newell agreed to guide Littlejohn and some Mormon
missionaries to Fort Hall on the Snake, Jules
packed up his furs and went along. They made the
trip in seventeen days, sold their furs to the Hudson Bay Company.

What really made up Jules's mind for him was
what Newell said to Joe Meek one day. Jules had

never forgotten it because he seemed to speak for all of them who had lived those years in the mountains.

"Come," said Newell to Meek. "We are done with this life in the mountains—done with wading in beaver dams, and freezing or starving alternately—done with Indian trading and Indian fighting. The fur trade is dead in the Rocky Mountains, and it is no place for us now, if ever it was. We are young yet, and have life before us. We cannot waste it here; we cannot or will not return to the States. Let us go down to the Willamette and take farms ... What do you say, Meek? Shall we turn American settlers?"

And Jules had not settled in the Willamette Valley, but had gone to Santa Fe and taken him a wife, Maria Montes, whose sister later married Levin Mitchell, now settled in a *placita* at the mouth of the Huerfano River down near El Pueblo, some twenty miles south. It was a village that Maria liked, not only because her sister was there, but because the Arkansas bottom west of the mouth of the Huerfano was rich black soil, thick with grass, and the banks of the river were dense with cottonwoods. The bottom there varied from half a mile to a mile in width and on the south, steep, thirty-foot bluffs of gravelly loam rose above the land like a fortress. In this wooded, protected place, the houses were not circled around a central plaza like those villages in New Mexico, but strung randomly along the river bottom, each little *placita* like a separate kingdom, but part of the whole.

Maria did not want to go there until she could be a land owner, a person of property, and Jules agreed with her. The new settlers on the Arkansas would stay there. There was talk of building and growing now that New Mexico and California belonged to the United States. There was a Mormon colony in Utah and Great Britain had given up its claim to the Oregon territory. People. Settlers, everywhere. The Pacific Railroad wanted to build a central route up the Arkansas, bridging the Atlantic seacoast with the Pacific, bringing people to the vast land between.

Moreaux had talked over these things with his friend Jacques Berthoud after the Arapaho had come into Sky Valley and taken the girls away. Jacques had told him a thing that he spoke of often to Maria ever since McGonigle and Angus McPherson had been killed by the Indians, and since Horne had come back with the only surviving Simmons girl.

"This valley," said Jacques, "is changed forever now, Jules. It is as if we have been betrayed by one among us and now we do not know who is friend and who is enemy."

"You mean Luke Newcastle?"

"But, yes, this Newcastle, yet he did not do anything to us that we did not allow to be done to us. We wanted the whiskey and he brought it to McGonigle and we paid for them to do this to us. We brought the Arapaho here and we will bring others who are just as bad."

"You think so, eh?" Jules had said.

"Ah, I believe, *mon ami*, and I know. We are proud of our little valley here and we boast of it down on the flat. So, the curious come to this place and they want what we have, so they come, too, or they take what they want and go away. Is it not so?"

"There is room for many," said Jules feebly.

"Perhaps, but some would say that we are already too many. And, maybe this is not our valley, but Horne's. He is the one who found it and he is the one who makes the others nervous. I think as long as Horne casts his shadow over this place, we are just guests, eh? This is what I think."

Jules had thought about that a lot and Jacques had moved away. It was sad, because Berthoud had been Jules's closest friend. Now, he was in the Arkansas Valley, maybe in El Pueblo, or in one of the *placitas*, and Jules thought that maybe he was right to leave when he did.

Dan Reinhardt had built his cabin above Horne's place and this worried Jules. Reinhardt was backed up against the walls of the valley and if he staked out a section of land, it would surely encroach on Horne's territory. It seemed almost deliberate now that he thought about it. There were other places Reinhardt could have chosen. Better ones, maybe.

Jules swung onto the trail leading to Reinhardt's and wondered if he was doing the right thing. He was going to tell Reinhardt a lie and maybe Reinhardt would believe him and go away. If he did not believe the lie, then Horne would be in more danger than he was now. If Horne lived.

The sun rose, but the clouds held and the snow was not too bright. Jules saw the tracks in the trail leading to Reinhardt's and was curious. Some were yesterday's and some were fresh and the snow was steaming where one of the horses had urinated and there was fresh mule dung smoking in a pile, like a marker in the wilderness. He counted four mules and two horses. At least two men, then, going to see the German in the dead of winter. There was more to wonder about now, and Jules squinted in the wan light as he followed the tracks that had churned the trail only moments before.

When he rode into the clearing, he saw the smoke rising from Reinhardt's chimney, saw the mules standing with their panniers empty, their lead ropes drooping. Two saddled horses stood hipshot at the hitch-rail, bedrolls behind the cantles, saddlebags bulging.

"Ho, Reinhardt!" called Moreaux, and he saw the door to the cabin open and a man's face appear behind the cloud of steam from the breath of the horses and mules.

"Moreaux?"

"Moreaux," said Jules.

He rode closer, reined up the paint, halted a few feet from the hitch-rail.

"You got business here?"

"I have some news for you, Reinhardt."

Reinhardt stepped out of the cabin, ducking to clear the doorway. He is a big man, thought Jules. Bigger than Horne, even, younger. His wool shirt clung to his torso like skin, the elkhorn buttons under strain, his suspenders stretched to the limit. He was a blond man, with piercing blue eyes. His hair was unkempt, flattened from wearing a hat, reaching almost to his broad shoulders. His body tapered to his hips, his legs were long and straight, visible under the heavy duck trousers he wore.

"Light down, then, and let's hear it."

Jules dismounted, surprised that Reinhardt would issue the invitation. He draped the pony's reins over the rail, spun them around twice and stepped toward the cabin. Reinhardt was already inside, the door open a crack. Moreaux stomped his boots, entered, and closed the door. The heat from the stone fireplace blasted him, made the room warm as summer.

"You want a drink, Moreaux?"

Jules shook his head, looked at the two men sitting at the table near the cookstove. Reinhardt pulled up a fourth chair, sat down and indicated an empty one for the Frenchman. Jules unbuttoned his coat, sat down. The two Mexicans smiled crookedly at him. One of them picked up the bottle and poured himself a drink, pushed the bottle towards Jules.

Jules shook his head again, looked at the two men carefully, then scanned the room. Coats lay in front of the fire, steaming, one of them Reinhardt's. The cabin was simple, stocked with traps, rifles, pistols, foodstuffs; a bunk, a footstool, a big chair covered with a buffalo robe; lamps and lanterns, wood for the fire. The cabin appeared solid, the chinking making it tight against the blowing of the winds, the chill of winter.

Reinhardt poured himself a drink and regarded Moreaux with a look of arrogance.

"This'll take the cold out of a man," said the German. "You have rid far?"

"From Horne's cabin," said Moreaux.

"Ah, and how did you find Mister Horne?"

"He is well," said Moreaux, telling the lie. "He has been shot, but it was only a scratch."

"And why do you tell me this?" asked Reinhardt bluntly.

"You know why, Reinhardt." Jules didn't flinch under Dan's withering gaze.

"Maybe. I—I did not shoot to kill."

Moreaux did not believe him. "Such a man is hard to kill."

Reinhardt looked at the two Mexicans, who smiled at him idiotically. Jules studied the German's face, saw the granite in it, the coldness of iron beneath his pale complexion. If there was a heart beating in that massive chest, Jules couldn't hear it in the silence of the room.

"I thought you killed Horne," said one of the Mexicans.

"So did I," said Reinhardt. "He looked dead enough. Maybe near to dying."

39

"Maybe this Frenchman he is *mentiroso*, eh?" said the Mexican.

Jules felt his face go hot, the flush of anger rise in his cheeks.

"I do not lie," said Moreaux. He looked at the two Mexicans again, realized that there was something familiar about them.

"I do not know," said the Mexican. "What do you think, Pedro?"

"Maybe he lies," said Pedro. *"No importa."*

"I know you," said Moreaux. "You are from El Pueblo."

The two Mexicans laughed in unison.

"Jules, meet Luis Delgado and Pedro Garcia. They bring news of El Pueblo."

Now Jules knew their names and knew he was right about their being from El Pueblo. But why were they here?

"What is this news?" asked Moreaux, dreading the answer.

"There is no more pueblo," said Delgado, looking into his half-filled glass of whiskey.

"It is gone," said Garcia. "Everyone dead." Then, he laughed and Jules knew he had never heard a more chilling sound. Delgado laughed, too, and Reinhardt smirked, rocked back in his chair.

"Chief Blanco's Muache Utes and some Jicarilla come through the gates of Pueblo on Christmas Eve last and killed damned near everybody," said Reinhardt.

"All but four," said Delgado, a swarthy man in his thirties with a stocky build, round face, a thick brush of moustache, and cheeks ruddy from the drink—as if they had been smeared with rouge. Garcia was larger, thinner, with a lean, hatchet face, a thin moustache, and a half inch of beard from ear to ear like a picture frame. Garcia's mouth was thin, while Delgado's was pudgy, almost seraphic, eternally pouting as if he had just sucked on a lemon.

"Blanco, he took some captives, too," said Garcia smugly. "One was a woman, but they killed her later."

Moreaux was stunned. He swore softly and the Mexicans laughed again.

"What about . . . the other villages?" Jules asked. "What about Huerfano?"

"Maybe you ought to have a drink, Moreaux," said Reinhardt, "and I'll tell you the whole story. You got kinfolk down there?"

"I—my wife, she . . . a sister. . . ."

"Maybe she is dead, too," said Delgado. "It doesn't make any difference. The Utes got their revenge on the whites and that makes it better for us."

"What do you mean?" asked Jules, dazed that such a thing had happened. He dreaded hearing the rest of the story, dreaded telling Maria what he had learned.

"Shut up," said Reinhardt to Delgado. "This is none of Moreaux's business."

Delgado's eyes flashed, but he said nothing. Angrily, he poured more whiskey into his glass.

"You tell me, Reinhardt," said Jules. "Tell me what happened at El Pueblo."

"Sure, Moreaux," said the German. "But first you tell me about Horne. I saw him go down. He was a dead man. If not right then, pretty soon."

Moreaux licked dry lips. The room suddenly seemed to close in on him. The two Mexicans fixed him with hard black stares. Reinhardt's eyes flickered with a look of pure hatred.

"You tell us the truth, Frenchman," said Garcia, "or maybe we kill you."

Pedro drew a pistol, a single-shot percussion, short-barreled .44 that filled his hand.

Garcia cocked the pistol, shoved the snout close to Moreaux's face. He grinned and his hand was steady.

Jules felt the sweat break out on his forehead.

"I think you will sing a different song, eh, Frenchman?"

Moreaux cleared his throat and tried hard to breathe without trembling. He looked into the blackness of the pistol barrel, thought about other times when he had faced death. Then, he had only himself to worry about, and nothing much to lose. It was easy to be brave, ten, fifteen years ago. But, now, he wondered if he was not a coward after all, because Jules Moreaux did not want to die—not for a man he had once known, but really did not know very well.

Not for Jackson Horne.

•CHAPTER 5•

HORNE AWOKE IN THE MORNING, RAVENOUS. THE cabin was still, the fire flickering, making the shadows dance on the log walls. He watched the room take on shape, waver as the shadows changed, move, disappear only to reappear again. He thought of yesterday and began to put together the pieces. He knew that Jules Moreaux had come after he was shot, that he had likely brought him home to Mary Lee. He remembered her, too, the burning in his wrist, the acrid smell of his own flesh on fire.

His arm hurt and his shoulder throbbed. Sweat sleeked his forehead and he realized he was wearing woolens that he had not had on the day before when he went out along his trapline. So, the woman had undressed him, put underwear on him. He listened, heard her out at the stables, taking care of Dancer, Tony, Stepper, and the mules. The clang of a pail against wood sounded reassur-

ing and the whicker of Tony brought a faint smile
to his lips. One of the mules snorted and whistled
and he looked at the boarded up windows and
wished he had glass in them so that he could see
out.

He struggled to rise, felt the weakness assail
him. Some starch had gone out of him, he figured.
He saw the bandage on his wrist, felt his shoulder.
It, too, was wrapped in softened cloth and stank
of horse medicant. Good enough for the likes of
him. He had used the salve before, on nicks and
cuts. It kept the flies off, anyways.

Horne lay back down, waited for Mary Lee to
return. He heard the tick of a pot on the stove and
saw steam rising from it. The cabin seemed empty
without her and he realized he had gotten used to
her.

He moved his wrist, felt pain shoot up his arm.
But he could move it and he knew he would heal.
Heal quicker than Mary Lee was healing. He
thought of the last time he had told her to go back
to her folks. It was a subject that came up a lot
after she took up with him, but he hadn't prodded
her in some time. He had wanted to, but the last
time he took her to McGonigle's, he knew it was
no use. He saw the way her parents looked at her,
the way everyone looked at her, oddly, knowing
she had shared Red Hawk's blanket and had been
violated by those murdering braves who killed
Caleb McGonigle and little Angus McPherson.

"Now'd be a good time to make peace with your
folks," he told her that day. "Maybe get some
heavy things off your chest."

She looked at him sharply, then over to her parents, who were standing on the porch of their
home right across the road from the trading post.
Elizabeth and Louis looked like statues, their faces
expressionless, drawn and pale.

"They would never understand," Mary Lee said quietly, and Horne knew what she meant. But it didn't change things. She wasn't his woman. She was only nineteen and she had those scars inside her that he couldn't heal. Some of his own hadn't healed yet. Maybe never would.

After Mary Lee took up with him, she slept curled up on the bear rug in front of the hearth. Horne gave her blankets out of pity, but he seldom spoke to her, nor she to him. He noticed that she made careful definition of which was woman's work, which was his. She did not tend to his stock, but she kept the cabin swept up, and washed the dishes. She asked him if she could have some of the deer hides stacked in the shed and he nodded in assent. He watched her brain-tan them, make herself a skirt and a pair of leggings. She did not show him the tiny garments she made and kept hidden. He would know soon enough about the seed she carried within her, know when her belly ripened like a gourd ready to pop. For now, this was her secret.

"You learnt a lot when you was with Red Hawk," he said to her one day.

"More than I can rightly say," she snapped at him, and then he saw her blush and knew what she was talking about without her saying the words. It was an embarrassment to both of them.

The door opened and Mary Lee tramped inside the cabin, stamping her feet to shake off the snow. Vagrant flakes of snow blew in after her, swirled around her as she shook her shawl. Snow clung to her braids, glistened in her forelock like jewels as she moved toward the fire in the hearth.

"You're awake," she said, rubbing red hands before the flames, batting her eyelashes.

"Yep," said Horne. "You took care of the stock."

"I did."

"You talked to Moreaux?"

"He didn't say much."

"He know who shot me?"

Mary Lee sucked in a quick breath, shot a glance at him from under hooded eyes.

"He said he didn't."

Horne grunted.

"You hungry, Horne?" she asked.

"I am some," he admitted.

"You want meat? I've got water on for broth."

"I better not have broth," he said. "It might come back up."

"I got to look at your wounds."

"You undressed me?"

"You know I did."

"Yeah," he said softly, and lay back on his bed, looking up at the beamed ceiling. He heard her scurrying around, banging a pot on the stove, stirring something with a wooden spoon. He was dog-tired, weary from what had been taken out of him. His mouth tasted leaden, dry. He wondered how much blood he had lost. It could have been worse. If Jules hadn't come up on him like that. . . .

She brought a wooden bowl, heaped with something that resembled a thick pudding.

"What is it?" he asked.

"Mush I made from cornmeal and broth," she said, and he noticed her face was dry now, her hair still wet. She sat on the edge of the bed, holding the spoon and bowl in her hands.

"I ain't no baby," he grumbled.

"I think you ought to keep that arm quiet," she said.

"I can eat one-handed," he argued.

"I don't mind feeding you. It's hot. There's some grease in the mush to give it taste."

Her talking irritated him for some reason. He kept thinking of Red Hawk and he wondered if he was jealous. Maybe he was, but he had no cause. Mary Lee wasn't his woman. She just acted like she was and that maybe galled him, too.

He scrooched up on the bed, leaned back against the headboard. A twinge of pain shot through his wounded arm and he grimaced slightly.

"See?" she taunted, dipping the spoon into the mush, and shoving it toward him defiantly.

Horne pouted, but she pried his mouth open with the spoon, forced the gruel inside. He gasped as the mush burned his mouth. He worried it around inside, saying, "Ah, ah, ah," until it cooled. He swallowed and the taste was good. He smelled coffee. It was a good smell, made him even hungrier.

His arm throbbed at the shoulder, but he ignored it as he dutifully ate the grease-laden mush. He thought it might stay down.

"That coffee fit to drink yet?" he asked.

"I think so. Get this inside you first."

"Hell, I'm dry swallerin' now, woman."

"You need your strength. The coffee's your reward for eating."

"You got the upper hand, I reckon," he said.

Mary Lee laughed mirthlessly.

"I guess that makes you fret," she said. "You men don't like women taking care of you."

Horne didn't answer. He wasn't stepping in that snare. The woman was smart. She could get you into the briar patch if you weren't careful. Mary Lee was more patient than most, but she did scatter hen's eggs in a man's path. You could hardly walk along without breaking one now and again.

· CHAPTER 6 ·

THE MUSH DID NOT STAY DOWN. NOW, THE CABIN smelled of sickness and Horne shivered with cold under woolen blankets and a heavy buffalo robe. His eyes seemed to sink in their sockets and glazed over as if they had been rubbed with sandpaper. When Mary Lee touched his forehead, she felt the fire raging in his flesh. She poured water into him, held him in her arms to keep him upright and let it trickle from the spout of the porcelain pitcher onto his parched lips, down his arid throat.

"Horne," she said, "you must keep the liquid down."

"Jim? That you?" he replied, and she knew he was delirious.

She rubbed snow on his chest and belly to bring the fever down. And she lay next to him to take away the chills—he was shaking so hard his teeth clattered like dice in a tin cup. She looked at the wound in his shoulder, saw that it was infected, and she bathed it with boiled water and put the salve in it, wrapped it loosely with fresh bandage made from an old petticoat she no longer wore.

"Got your horses, did they, Bill?" said Horne, and looked glassy into the distance. There was a strange husk to his voice that Mary Lee had never heard before and she lay him back on his bed, rubbed his fevered forehead with a caressing palm.

"Oh, Horne," she pleaded, "can't you get well?"

"I make 'em to be Blackfeet," said Horne, and closed his eyes as if he was drifting back to some time in the mountains, far away from her, far away from the present.

"I hope it's cool there," she sighed, and pulled the blankets and robe over him as she fought back the tears of frustration.

Horne's breathing grew deep and labored and she knew he was locked into dreams he had dreamed before. She had heard some of this talk before when he was sleeping and she was lying awake before the fire wondering what kind of life he had lived before he had come to the valley, what kind of violent, terrible life he had survived.

Pedro Garcia and Luis Delgado were men who looked for opportunity wherever they went and they didn't much like working for a living. Over the years they had attracted a following of other malcontents. They had done some trapping, but had learned that greenhorns were fairer game than the beaver and a lot easier to skin. When the Santa Fe Trail opened up between Santa Fe and St. Louis, they were among the bandits who raided the emigrant trains for profit. Later, they moved to the Rio Grande Valley below Santa Fe, competing with the Kiowas, Comanches and Arapahos who were killing settlers and running off stock.

They were idling away at Bent's Fort in 1848, when the firm of Bent, St. Vrain and Co. went under, deeply indebted to Pierre Chouteau Jr. and Co., their St. Louis agents. They watched, the next year, when William Bent closed the gates of his fort and set fire to the magazine. The powder made quite a blow, but didn't do much damage to the rest of the fort. Still, it was time to move on. Bent went to Big Timbers to trade with the Cheyenne and Arapaho and Garcia and Delgado went south to Taos, passing through Pueblo and Greenhorn, the settlements along the Arkansas.

They heard unsettling stories of travelers at their old stamping grounds along the old Oregon Trail up the Platte. Emigrants spoke of finding lots of graves, cattle carcasses, scattered pieces of iron from hundreds of abandoned wagons, burned to drive out the cholera and because there was no grass to feed the pulling stock. People were now using the Arkansas as a travel route and the Mexicans saw a new wave of sheep to be sheared. People streamed toward California with picks and pans and dreams of gold to be picked up from the streams and blasted out of rock.

The Pueblo was abandoned by the summer of 1850 and that's when Delgado and Garcia made their headquarters along Fountain Creek. From there, they could range far and wide, robbing emigrants at will, just as they had done along the Santa Fe and Oregon trails in years past.

The life they chose was not without its perils. Indians preyed on the emigrants as well, and the outlaw band had to fight off Arapaho pillagers as they rode toward Greenhorn to rob the villagers of corn and cattle. The next year, Apaches came to the Arkansas Valley, south of Greenhorn, to lie in wait for travelers.

Garcia and Delgado kept the Apaches stirred up. It was good for business. Often they would act as guides and rob the wagon trains themselves, leaving the hapless survivors as easy prey for the Apaches. They narrowly missed encountering Kit Carson when he came through from Fort Laramie, driving forty or fifty head of horses to trade to the emigrants.

The Apaches were competition, but they were also good for business. Often, the Mexicans dressed as Apaches and laid the blame on the Indians as they raided wagon trains and took their booty back to Fountain Creek, unmolested by pursuers. Meanwhile, the Indians thought that the settlers at Greenhorn on the St. Charles River were the competition and they began a series of raids on that settlement and others along the river. They killed a man in Greenhorn in the summer of 1851 and attacked another settlement, carrying off provisions, stock, money, and a captive. The next summer, a band of Navajos, Jicarilla Apaches and Utes, on their way to battle with the Kiowas and Arapahos, attacked Greenhorn again, stealing horses and cattle, finishing off the town.

Delgado and Garcia saw these things happening, and heard the threats that the Indians would drive all white men out of the Arkansas Valley. This news was offset as more emigrants surged up from Taos and Santa Fe and from the east, driven by dreams of riches inspired by the advent of a steam railroad. In March of 1853, Congress approved a bill for the survey of a proposed central route to the Pacific. The rails would be laid up the Arkansas and Huerfano rivers and cross the Sangre de Cristo Pass.

The band of Mexican outlaws had almost decided to leave for greener pasturage when this news reached them. Delgado and Garcia had seen the settlements disappear one by one, abandoned to the stillness of winter early in 1853. They rode through ghost towns where the wind hummed in vacant log *placitas* and adobe rooms infested with rats and rabbits, their courtyards stirring with skeletal tumbleweeds, their roofs caved-in, their windows like the vacant sockets of skulls.

The Pueblo had withstood the ravages of time and the buildings still stood. Settlers occupied them and others came and built homes along the Huerfano. Grants were issued and New Mexican officials began touting the region. More and more emigrants began to settle into the Pueblo and *placitas*, each one a small fort, began to dot the landscape.

But the Utes had been lied to and tormented for too long, decimated by starvation, slaughtered by Arapahos and Cheyennes while the government looked the other way, and as the band of one thousand Muaches dwindled, Chief Blanco finally went on the warpath.

Jules Moreaux listened in horror as Luis Delgado recounted what had happened that Christmas Eve when the Utes had gone on the rampage.

"It was pretty quiet on the Arkansas," said Delgado, "all that week. Pedro, he sent some men with three cartloads of goods we stole up to trade with the Arapahos at Bijou Basin on the Platte-Arkansas divide. We saw people leaving Huerfano village with goods, and some other people from that settlement on the mouth of the St. Charles went out hunting. Hell, we had plenty, we did not bother them. Somebody was bringing corn into Huerfano. Me and Pedro, we went hunting, too.

"Up on Coal Creek I saw a Ute sneaking along

and when I made sign to him, he rode off quick. I saw a lot of fresh pony tracks. Pedro, he rode on up the creek and saw where many horses had crossed the night before and he said we better ride on back to Pueblo. That Ute I saw was painted for war."

Pedro poured from the whiskey bottle, emptied it into three glasses. He offered what was left in the bottle to Moreaux, but Jules shook his head.

"A lot of your friends got killed, I think," said Garcia. "You lucky you was up here, huh? That is what I think."

"We have heard nothing of this," said Moreaux.

"You do not believe me? Luis, you tell him what we found out, eh? I think this Frenchman don't want to hear the truth."

"I want to hear the truth," said Moreaux. "But, we have heard nothing of any Utes attacking the Pueblo."

"You're hearing it now," said Reinhardt coldly. "Go on, Luis. Tell it all. . . ."

A man named Dick Wootten had also seen the tracks on Coal Creek. He did not follow them, but rode to the fort, hell bent for leather, the steam of his breath scattering like broken cobwebs in the wind. He, too, had seen the lone Indian painted for war, knew that he was Ute. At Pueblo an old man rushed out to meet him.

"Dick," he yelled, "I saw tracks on the river. Pony tracks, a million of 'em."

"So, they crossed the river, did they?"

"A passel, I swear."

"They're probably close by, then, waiting to attack," said Wootten, between lung-searing breaths. His side ached with the same fire of muscles straining for oxygen.

"You stay inside, old man," said Wootten.

"Don't let nobody in, no Injuns anyways. I'm meet-in' George McDougal and some others what was with me and we're ridin' on to warn the folks at Huerfano."

"I'm plumb scared," said the old man.

"I'll pass the word. You keep powder and ball handy."

Wootten rode off, and soon, people began coming to the fort, which was no more than a small square of baked adobe, circular bastions at its corners, with walls no more than eight foot high in any section. The yard was surrounded by a dozen little rooms. In other times, the rooms would be dwellings for three or four Taos women and as many Indian women from various tribes. These were mothers of dirty tykes who gave good promise, wrote George Frederick Ruxton, the dapper little Englishman who had passed through the Pueblo, "of peopling the river with a sturdy race of halfbreeds, if all the little dusky buffalo-fed urchins who played about the corral of the fort arrived scatheless at maturity." The people lived entirely on wild game and were without bread most of the year since they grew little corn. When they ran low on meat, they rode to the mountains, pulling pack animals which they brought back loaded with buffalo or elk or deer meat. Game was scarce near the Pueblo and buffalo had long since vanished from the prairie lands. But they could always find game in the high country, particularly in one vast mountain valley they called *Bayou Salade*.

It was Christmas Eve and there was celebrating to do, Indians or no Indians. It was quiet, and the Utes didn't come. The men got up a card game and it lasted all night. Three men from Baca's settlement sat in on the game, José Ignacio Valencia, Rumaldo Cordova and Tanislado de Luna. Juan

Blas Martin's wife, Chepita Miera, was the only
woman in the fort. She was going to move out of
the fort at first light and her goods were already
packed and loaded in Rumaldo's wagon, which
was just outside the gate to the fort. She waited
patiently until the game was over, nervous, jump-
ing at every alien sound.

The small celebration ended just before daybreak. José Ignacio Valencia, his coat and trousers
rumpled, teetered until he got his balance and
walked through the gate into the chill of morning,
headed for his cabin at Baca's. When he got home,
he saw that he had left his knife at the fort. He
staggered back in that direction, still befuddled
from drink, despite the cold.

Young Benito Pais, whom they called Guero,
rode out of the fort to fetch some milk at Baca's.
He shivered in the winter chill, drew deeper into
his ragged coat made out of sheep and buffalo
scraps so that it resembled a patchwork quilt,
white and black with no rhyme nor reason to the
pattern of hide and hair. He crossed the gravel
ford at Fountain Creek and heard a shrill whistle.
He looked up toward the *loma* north of Baca's
adobe house. There, atop the bluff, he saw a line
of mounted Indians silhouetted against the cream-
yellow sky of daybreak. He clapped his heels into
the horse's flanks and galloped to Baca's, yelling
"Indians, Indians!"

At about the same time as José was staggering
back towards the fort and Guero was riding away
from the Pueblo, the boy, Felipe Cisneros, stepped
outside the fort to bring the horses in. He saw that
the cattle had not been brought in the night before
either. He did not know where the cattle-herder
was. The corral was empty of stock. He climbed
the *loma* above the fort and looked all around. No
horses, or cattle. Alarmed, he broke into a run,

hurtled down the bluff to Baca's. As he reached
the foot of the hill he saw an Indian riding slowly
up to Baca's adobe. Felipe hunched over and
scrambled into a ravine. He ran down to the timber along the banks of the muddy, slow-flowing
Arkansas and hid like a frightened rabbit in the
brush.

Marcelino Baca heard Guero Pais yelling the
alarm. He donned a muslin shirt and slipped on
dark duck trousers and dashed out to the jacal
cabins behind his house and woke up the women
sleeping there. These were the wives of Valencia,
Cordova and de Luna. *"Andale, andale!"* he whispered. "Hurry!"

"What is it?" asked a puffy-eyed *Señora* Valencia.

"Indios sobre la loma. Muchos, con caballos."

"Maybe they are friendly."

"I think maybe so, but you come with me to the
house. Quick, quick!"

Inside the house, Marcelino repeated his opti-
mistic opinion to José Barela.

"I think maybe they do not mean us harm," said
Baca. "They are just sitting up there on the bluffs.
Maybe they are going hunting at South Pass."

Barela, a wise old man, who knew much, shook
his head.

"I remember that a trader was killed at Apache
Creek a short while ago, Marcelino. Yes, it was
Blanco and his band of Ute Indians."

"Maybe if I went up there and talked to
them. . . ." said Baca.

"No!" shouted the old man. "Do not make
friends with the Indians or they'll kill us!"

Baca's face wrinkled into a scowl until it resembled wet leather and he spoke to the others.

"Close the house up tight, women! Men, get your
guns and make sure they are primed."

Moments later, Baca looked through a gunport chiseled below a shuttered window, saw Blanco himself riding up. There were more than a hundred Utes and a few Apaches behind him.

"That bastard is riding my best white horse," said Baca.

"That is so," said Barela. "We will go out now and meet with him. Take our rifles."

"Why?"

"Because they mean to shoot us here like barn mice," said the old man.

The women screamed softly, clutched at one another like demented pickpockets.

"Baca, you come out!" shouted Blanco in Spanish.

Baca and Barela stepped outside, their rifles held high across their chests. Baca went to the east of the house, Barela to the west, so that they did not stand together. There was an ominous sound as someone cocked a hammer, but Blanco held up his hand for silence. A mild breeze blew down from the *loma*, but it was as gelid as if it had blown down from the Sangre de Cristos and it rattled feathers and wing bones and leather pouches as it passed. The women inside the house began to wail and scream in terror.

"*Amigo,*" said Blanco in a voice full of friendliness, "*yo quiero a hablar contigo. Pongan los rifles. . . .*"

"Blanco, you thief," said Baca, "if you come one step closer, we'll blow your head off."

At that moment, Baca's little girl, Elena, broke from the house of screaming women and ran to her father, grabbed at his legs. He pushed her away with one callused and knobby brown hand and kept the rifle crooked in his arm pointed toward Blanco. Elena ran across the open to Barela, jabbering in baby-talk Spanish.

57

"Get back inside the house, little one," said Barela.

The little girl ran back to the house. Her mother, a full-blood Pawnee, rushed out to grab her, swearing at her in the Latin tongue. Then, she pulled her daughter inside by the arm and began whipping her. Elena's screams pierced the air.

"We will go, Baca. You take care," said Blanco. He lifted his hand and the one hundred-odd Indians followed him in silence. They rode past the corn crib and the cows and calves in the corral behind the house, but they never made a move to take anything of Baca's.

"They go without stealing," said Barela.

"The bastards have already stolen everything I own before the sun was up, old man."

"True."

"I am a poor man," said Baca simply.

The Utes and the Apaches headed toward the fort at El Pueblo.

• CHAPTER 7 •

L UIS DELGADO WIPED A GRIMY HAND ACROSS HIS mouth. Steam rose from the coats by the fire. Pedro threw more wood on while Reinhardt rolled a smoke. Moreaux licked dry lips, stared at Delgado's glittering eyes, knowing the man was enjoying it. He was like a cat toying with a half-dead mouse, pawing it one way, then the other, giving it the illusion of freedom, but ready to pounce at any moment if the mouse tried to escape.

"We heard them screaming at the fort," said Delgado, "and we heard them shooting. And then it was very quiet. When we rode up, we saw Barela, Cisneros and Baca riding up to see what had happened.

"They found José Valencia on the east side of the Fountain at the gravel ford. The Utes had chased him down there and killed him. He had bullet holes all through him and there wasn't much left of his face. We crossed the Fountain with them and here comes Juan Medina walking *zigzagueando* toward us, holding onto his belly, which looked like the mouth of a whale. His guts were spilling out all over his fingers, gray shining ropes, and you could smell his shit a hundred paces in all directions.

"Medina, he say, 'water, I have the thirst, give me water,' and Cisneros, he run back to the river and scooped up some water in his hands. Medina he took a drink of that cold water and said everybody at the fort was dead. He died then too and we left him there and rode to the gap, you know, *Puertocito*. . . ."

"I know," said Jules softly.

"At *Puertocito* we find that Navajo sumbitch, Guadalupe Vigil. He got an arrow in the back and it was sticking out like a big porkypine quill. He had another arrow stuck in one of his fingers like he had thrown up his hand to hold it back, you know." Delgado laughed harshly and Reinhardt smiled. Garcia stepped outside and they could hear his urine hiss as it hit the snow beyond the door. The cold air came into the cabin and the fire whipped in the fireplace and belched golden sparks up the chimney before Garcia came back in and slammed the door.

"We went on back to the fort and found three dead Utes lying on the frozen ground. They looked like big dolls some kid had thrown away."

"Was there no one alive?" croaked Moreaux.

"We thought everybody was dead," said Garcia, scraping the chair legs as he sat down, reached for his glass. His face was ruddy from the drink and the cold, the cheekbones burnished with a rosy flame. "There was a wagon sitting outside all loaded with trunks and furniture. We heard this moaning and looked on the other side. You tell him, Luis."

"You know Rumaldo Cordova, Moreaux?" asked Delgado.

"I know him," said Jules. "He is a friend to my brother-in-law."

"We see this bloody path from the chicken coop to the fort and then we see Rumaldo Cordova near the gate. He's sitting down and he's got his head hung over like he's drunk, but he's spitting blood and there is about a bowl of it between his legs, just floating there in a pool.

"Baca asked Rumaldo if he was hurt and then Rumaldo looked up and tried to say something, but no words come out. Baca asks him what had happened, and I laughed and told Baca that the man had been shot in the mouth and wasn't going to talk much.

"Then Rumaldo begins talking in sign and he tells us that Chepita is gone."

"She was his sister-in-law," said Moreaux.

"I know," said Delgado. "He said she was sitting in the wagon outside the gate waiting for him when the Utes came up and grabbed her. When Rumaldo ran out of the fort to help her one of the Indians shot him in the neck with an arrow. Another one came up and shot him in the mouth. He played dead and they started shooting everyone and chasing them."

"*Sacre Marie*," breathed Moreaux.

"That goddamned Rumaldo was a liar," said Garcia. "We talked later to Juan Cornejo, a kid, who had maybe twelve years, and he sang a different song, eh Luis?"

"This Juanito was one of the *huerfanos* from upriver who just walked down to the fort at the wrong time, looking for food or tobacco," replied Delgado. "An orphan, with no home and no family. He hid when the Utes rode up, but he saw what happened. Baca tried to shut him up, but we gave him some tobacco and he told us that it didn't happen like Rumaldo told it, that *cobarde*."

"Rumaldo was probably scairt real bad," offered Moreaux.

"He had soiled his pants, I think," said Delgado, laughing. He pulled out his pipe and filled the bowl with tobacco as if reliving those moments after the massacre. He lit it with a sulphur match and blew a ragged smoke ring toward the ceiling of the cabin. Moreaux sat there, rigid as slab oak, trying to picture the fort in his mind, how it must have looked that bleak morning, that terrible, bloody Christmas day.

These were people he knew, had known, and some of them were dead, or worse, held hostage by the Utes. He squeezed his eyes shut and wondered what he was going to say to his wife when he returned home. If he returned home. Somehow, he felt there was worse to come, for him, for all of those who lived in Sky Valley.

"This *huerfano*," Delgado went on, "he say that an Indian walked up to the fort on foot, alone, and asked for something to eat. Nobody would let him in, so he went away. A few minutes later, Blanco himself rode up and got off his horse. He said, 'Open the gate,' and Benito Sandoval and Rumaldo, they opened the gate. Then, Benito told Rumaldo, 'go ahead and shoot Blanco.'

"Rumaldo shook his head and told Benito, 'This is my friend,' and he pulled Blanco inside the fort like a fool; and the other Utes crowded up and followed him in, and they filled up the courtyard. Blanco grabbed Rumaldo's gun, jerked it out of his hands and shot Rumaldo in the mouth. One of the Utes picked up young Felix Sandoval, Juanito Cornejo saw it plain, and put him on a horse and some others rode him out of the fort. Then, one of the Indians who took Felix turned around and shot his father, Benito, right in the chest."

"Oh no," said Moreaux. "Not Benito. And, they took little Felix."

"We walked inside that courtyard and saw the others," said Delgado. "They were not pretty. There were some dead Utes, but we also saw Juan Blas Martin, and we had done some trading with him now and again, and Francisco Mestas, both dead."

"We found Manuel Lucero, too," said Garcia, "remember?"

"*Trujeque*, they called him," said Moreaux soberly. "Was he dead, too?"

"He was dead," said Delgado. "His fingers were wrapped around the handle of a flatiron in a death grip."

"Benito, he did not die right away," said Garcia. "We find him at the foot of a ridgepole. His fingerprints were all over the pole, red with his blood."

"That boy, Juanito, said that after Benito was shot, he grabbed his youngest son, what was his name, Pedro?"

"I don't know," said Garcia.

"Juan Isidro," said Moreaux. "He was the ringbearer at my sister's wedding."

"Well, that is real good to know," said Delgado. "Benito and the boy ran into the bastion. He locked the door, but the Utes were mad as devils and they tore the roof up and shot Benito through the top of his head. He killed two of them before they got him, though."

"And the boy?" asked Moreaux. "Juan Isidro would be only about seven years now."

"The Utes took him, too. He wasn't there and that's what Juanito Cornejo told us."

"Is that all?" asked Jules.

"They started picking up bodies, then, putting them in the wagons. We rode around, following Blanco's tracks, just to see where he was going. We ran into some men from the villages of Huerfano and St. Charles come to help bury the dead. They had found Joaquin Pacheco on the bank of the Arkansas, a half mile from El Pueblo. He was lanced so hard there were holes in the ground underneath him. They dug a big hole in front of the fort and buried five men in that one grave. They covered the graves with logs to keep the wolves from digging the dead men up and they left the dead Utes out for wolfmeat. They had a wake that night and a prayer vigil for the ones they couldn't find."

"Besides the boys and Chepita, who else was taken?" asked Moreaux.

"Juan Aragon and Tanislado de Luna. They're still looking for them, I think."

"Did you find out where the Utes went?" asked Jules.

"We know they made camp that night on Grape Creek, and they took Baca's corn on their way back, just as they meant to, all along. I heard they got into a fight with Arapahoes, but we got the hell out until the country settles down some. We'll go back in a week." Delgado smirked, then his face turned hard.

"You must now tell us about this Horne, whether he is dead or alive, if he is shot up bad enough to die pretty soon." There was no pity in Delgado's eyes, no mercy in his glare.

"I think he will live," said Moreaux and at that moment, he knew Horne had to live. "I think he just hit his head on a rock and is probably walking around now, looking for the man who shot him."

"All right, Moreaux," said Reinhardt, stubbing out the remains of his quirly in a clay bowl on the table, "maybe Horne's not dead, but I hit him in the head with the first shot and I think I got a lung on the second."

"Ah, the first shot only creased him," said Jules, enthusiastic in his conviction. "And the second shot was only a flesh wound in the shoulder."

"You swear?" asked Reinhardt, his blue eyes cold as agates and just as lifeless.

"I swear," said Jules.

Delgado smirked once again. Garcia snorted in disbelief.

Moreaux looked at each man and knew that he had to hold his head up and be strong if he was to get away from them alive. The two Mexicans reeked of blood. There was an animal smell about them that made his nostrils burn. Reinhardt was a puzzling man, but inside, he was just the same as the Mexicans. He was hard and cold and as merciless as a mountain avalanche.

"Moreaux, I got to tell you something," said Reinhardt. "This valley is growing fast. More and more folks are moving in here and that means trouble. We got to have law and order. But, we don't want outsiders telling us what to do. We are going to make a town here and have our own sheriff and judge and mayor. Horne doesn't fit in. He's not one of us."

"He was here first," Moreaux reminded him.

"That's just the point. He's stayed behind, while we've moved ahead. The others are with me on this: McPherson, Simmons, Winder, MacGregor, all of them. We don't want Horne here. Even your friend Jacques agrees with me and the others."

"Jacques?"

"Berthoud," interrupted Garcia. Jacques Berthoud. He is one of my men now. It was he who brought us up here to see your old friend Horne. Even now, he is probably at your home, speaking with your wife. He says you may want to make some money with us, eh?"

Jules felt his stomach swim with a queasy swirl. He fought to keep the surge of bile out of his throat as a wave of nausea threatened to engulf him. Jacques Berthoud? With the Mexicans? How? Why? How could this be?

"I do not understand," said Jules.

"Aha!" exclaimed Garcia. "There is much you do not understand. When the Utes and Apaches came through, they took all the horses and cows. Then, the Arapaho, they want their share, so they took the horses and cows from the Utes. Now, the people in the south want horses and cows. Jacques knows where there are horses. Many horses. He says he must tell Dan here what we are going to do and Dan will take care of Horne for us, saving us the trouble. Horne knows us, you see. Horne and us we are old friends, eh Luis?"

"You know Horne?" asked Moreaux, more bewildered than ever.

"Yes," hissed Delgado. "Pedro and him are old friends from Santa Fe. And me, I have known this man, too." The look on Delgado's face made Moreaux's innards draw up in fear. It was a look of purest hatred, like looking into the eyes of a coiled rattlesnake, like staring into the face of a homicidal madman.

"You are going to steal Horne's horses," Jules said. It was not a question. He knew. He also knew how highly Horne valued his horseflesh.

"We will, how you say, kill two *cordonices* with one stone," said Pedro Garcia, and he looked through Moreaux, into the empty distance that only he could see, like a man who had been carrying such a thought with him a long time.

"You'll have to kill him, then," said Moreaux.

"Maybe we have a better way," said Reinhardt, looking at the two Mexicans. Delgado and Garcia smiled. "You can help us. Join us. Help us make a town."

"If it means going against Horne, I can't," said the Frenchman.

"It means going with us, the town, with the Law."

"And who is to be the Law?" asked Moreaux.

"I will be the Law," said Reinhardt. "I *am* the Law."

• CHAPTER 8 •

HORNE DRIFTED IN AND OUT OF FEVERISH DREAMS, babbled in delirium, hallucinated. Sometimes he did not know when he was awake or asleep. At times, Mary Lee appeared to him as Bill Sublette or Nathaniel Wyeth, or Thomas Fitzpatrick. Men he had known. More than once, the woman who stood by his bed wore the hideous paint of the Blackfoot, her hair black as a coal pit, medicine feathers bristling in the odd, distorted light of dream.

Mary Lee Simmons rubbed his naked body with snow, brought to the cabin in a wooden pail whenever she felt the fever was high enough to cook his brain. There were times when his voice frightened her and she looked at him in puzzlement, wondering where his mind had taken him, where his spirit had gone for the moment.

She held him to her in the night, held him close to her own nakedness and wished he knew that she was there and wanted him so much. His body drew away her own coolness at those times and she was sure her fever matched his, she wished for him so. When he moved, her heart jumped and a childish fear replaced her desire. She knew she was taking advantage of his condition, but she rationalized that she was helping bring his fever down and that made her liberties not so much like sin, but only nursing and doctoring.

She kept his wounds clean and salved. She looked often for the tell-tale streaks of blue up his arm, but never saw them and knew that he did not have gangrene. The scab on his wrist hardened into a rough, bumpy shell and the wound in his shoulder lost its puffiness and stopped leaking pus onto the bandage.

Horne's fever broke two days later. He awoke, his brow cool, his bedclothes soaked with night-sweat. The odor of ammonia permeated the cabin, mingled with the steamy aroma of clothing and lye soap from a boiling iron pot on the cookstove.

Mary Lee approached the bed where Horne sat up, blinking at the light, squinting through the steamcloud that hung in the room. His face was brushy with beard, his lips cracked from the fever. His eyes were no longer vacant or dilated, his skin was no longer pale and gray.

"You're some better this morning," she said.

"I feel like a bear what's been in hibernation."

"You're hungry, then."

"I am."

"You want broth, or can you hold down some meat?"

"Both," he grinned and Mary Lee smiled.

"You better wash up, then," she said. "I kept you clean as I could, but you still stink."

Horne sniffed deep. He moved his arm, winced

69

at the twitch of pain that coursed through his muscles.

"I don't smell anything but wash and lye soap," he said.

"I'll set out some clothes for you, put a pan on so you can bathe yourself."

Horne watched her move into the steam. Her outline blurred and he heard the clank of a pot, the slosh of water from a wooden pail. He rubbed his face, worked his left hand. The wrist was less sore than the shoulder; both were still bandaged.

He wolfed down the broth, thick with wild onions, barley, chunks of venison, cracked corn. Mary Lee sat on the edge of the bed, watching him, but he didn't look up until he was finished.

"More?" she asked.

"You put a heap of pepper into it."

"Good for your blood," she said.

"I'll have another, then. Don't be shy with the meat."

She laughed, took his bowl. Horne looked around the cabin, saw that she had kept it neat. There was nothing out of place. He ate the second bowl slower than the first, looked at her, wondering what new secrets she had to keep from him. He was naked and he knew she had shared his bed with him. He couldn't say how he knew, but someone had been in bed with him, someone soft and lithe, and he knew that—knew it from those lucid intervals when the fever was raging in him like a burning forest.

Horne handed her the empty bowl, rubbed his naked belly.

"Good," he said. "Now either fetch me some clothes or I'll hop out of bed and . . ."

"No! I'll get them," she said quickly, and her face went from alabaster to ruddy so fast he almost laughed.

"Did I miss much?" Horne asked as he pulled on his skins. Mary Lee deliberately had her back to him as she wrestled the dishes in the tin pan of hot soapy water.

"Two days, Horne."

"Visitors?"

Mary Lee's back straightened. Horne caught it. He tried not to miss things like that.

"No," she said tightly, as if it was a lie she didn't want to tell.

"No matter. You kept 'em off me."

She turned around as he pulled on his boot moccasins. Her hands were mittened with suds.

"Nobody came," she said again.

"Pass by, then." He cocked his head as he pulled the laces tight, snugged the leather against his shin.

"Horne, you're no damned good."

"I know a lie when I hear it. Little or big, white or black."

Her face flushed with color again. It was one of her most becoming features, Horne thought.

"Maria Moreaux stopped by when I was out feeding the stock. She—she said Jules wanted to pack up and move down to the Pueblo. She didn't know why. In the dead of winter. Jacques Berthoud was up, gone now. Jules wouldn't tell her anything and she was upset."

"I thought the Frenchie left for good. Maybe Jules wants to go with him."

"Marie didn't want to go."

"No, a woman wouldn't want to leave her home. Most women," he said sarcastically.

"Don't you start on me, Horne."

"I won't," he said.

"You goin' somewhere?" she asked as he stood up.

71

"Just want to see how my arm feels out in the cold. I'll look at the stock."

He strapped on his pistol, left his coat on the wall.

"You stay close, Horne."

He looked at her as if he was going to say something, but she turned back to her dishpan and he shrugged. He wasn't used to staying inside with Mary Lee during the day. He didn't know if he could stand it for very long. She had sure gotten bossy all of a sudden. Maybe she had a right, taking care of him like she did.

The air was crisp and the sun was trying to fight its way through clouds. Horne's breath made a ghostly cloud as he walked to the corral. The horses nickered, stamped the ground at his approach. He spoke to them, crawled through the rail fence. They came up to him and he rubbed their muzzles, patted their necks. The mules stood surly, hipshot, in one corner of the corral, all gimlet-eyed, their coats long-shagged with winter hair.

Dancer nibbled at his palm, Tony rubbed against his good shoulder. Stepper stood behind the other two, a roan gelding he had brought up from winter quarters to see how he managed in the mountain cold. Stepper had some Arabian in him, the small feet would be good on narrow sheep trails, Horne figured, if he had the lungs and the stamina to withstand the thin air. Dave Sheppers, his foreman at the ranch in LaPorte, had said Stepper might make a mountain horse, sure of foot, strong of limb, if he got used to the altitude. Stepper was almost three years old and Horne had bought him as a yearling from a Missouri man at Taos. There was a lot about the horse that he liked, his odd markings, the gray-blue coloration, the small feet, the lean frame, the barrel chest. A year on grain and tall grass had put some meat on the horse, but he still had that lean look about him and his chest had filled out. He was broke to the saddle, but Horne had not ridden him in the mountains yet. It was something he meant to do before spring.

Horne checked the grain supply, smelled the familiar musty aroma of dried corn and oats, the leather of the tack room inside the barn, the horse manure in the sparse straw. Mary Lee had kept things neat and tidy, he noticed, doing work he usually did for himself. She deserved a compliment, maybe.

He walked on through the barn, climbed the fence to the back corral. It was empty, the snowy ground unspoiled except by his own footprints. He walked back to the creek and watched it for a while, listened to its mindless gurgle. He checked the trough he had built to carry water to his stock. It was solid, no leaks, the gate valve turned off, wrapped in buffalo hide to keep it from freezing.

He looked up through the trees, feeling light-headed. His arm began to throb. He tried to lift it and pain shot through the nerve-ends like bullets of fire. The arm would be no good for a while, but he could move it. He had wondered if he might not have lost a tendon. He felt the muscles, the biceps, to see if they had started turning to flab. Nothing noticeable yet and he vowed to work the arm every day for as long as he could stand it. The wrist hurt now, too, but not much. He felt the scab underneath the bandage. It was as hard as a piece of horn.

He had not wanted to think about the man who had shot him. But the thought came back now, and he remembered how the man had made the trap clang against the rock, waited for him. A damned bushwhacker. A sneak. The man must have thought he had done the job, or else he had heard Jules Moreaux coming and didn't want to be seen. Horne thought of the men he knew in the valley, wondered if it could have been any of them. Not likely. Maybe one of the newcomers. He hadn't run into them yet, but he knew there were more settlers up here now. One had built a cabin above his place, far enough away not to bother about, maybe. Horne didn't know the man, had never seen him.

Lou Simmons could have hired someone to put Horne's lamp out. That thought occurred to him. What was Berthoud doing up here this time of year? He didn't trust the Frenchie, but he didn't think he was a backshooter. Maybe Berthoud had gotten lonesome for his friend Jules. Horne knew it wasn't Jules who shot him. Jules would have faced him if there had been a reason. Jules Moreaux wasn't the kind to kill a man without reason and in the dark or from behind a bush.

Moreaux might know who did the shooting, though. Horne thought that was likely.

Maybe when he could move his arm without having his head fill up with shooting stars he would ride over to Moreaux's and ask him a question or two.

It wasn't over yet.

Whoever had shot him was likely to try again.

Horne meant to see that he got his chance.

• CHAPTER 9 •

JACQUES BERTHOUD TUGGED THE DIAMOND HITCH tight, rammed a fist up into the mule's belly to take out the swell. The mule humped and Jacques jerked the rope tight, knotted it. He hefted the canvas bag full of furs, looped the handle over the opposite side of the pannier, snugged it up. He went to the other side, slung the other satchel up, secured it to the forks of the other side. He threw a tarpaulin over the pannier and lashed it to the mule with no wasted motion.

"Done," he said to Garcia, who stood by the other mule, blowing on his bare hands.

"Pancho, let's ride," Garcia said to Jacques.

"Where is Luis?"

"He will find us," said Pedro laconically.

Jacques looked around. Luis Delgado had been there earlier when they were saddling their horses. So had Dan Reinhardt. But now, both were gone. Jacques didn't like it. He didn't like these

75

men, much, but he had made his choice. Times were poor and a man had to live.

"There's not enough fur here to feed one man, I think," said Jacques. "We are three, with a long ride back to Pueblo."

"Do not worry about that, my friend. We take the furs, but we pick up something better, eh? Horses."

This was the first Jacques had heard about horses. The Mexicans had not told him much, nor had Reinhardt spoken more than two words to him. He had brought the Mexicans up here to see Reinhardt and he knew their coming had something to do with Jackson Horne, but that was all. Then Garcia had told him to try to talk Moreaux into joining them, going back with them to the Fountain.

Moreaux was going back with them. Jacques knew he was worried about his sister-in-law. He was worried about something else, too, but he wasn't talking. That was unlike Jules. He and Moreaux had known each other a long time, since the trapping days. Jacques had joined Chouteau's American Fur when he was fifteen, had stayed five years in the mountains. When he left the last rendezvous he was only twenty years old, Jules was nineteen. Jules had not looked more than his age, but Jacques had aged. He looked thirty then, he looked fifty now. He had the swarthy olive skin of his Mediterranean forebears, hair black as anthracite; brown button-eyes that wallowed in sockets too big for them; a neck grown thick from a goiter that he kept concealed with a bandanna perpetually shrouding it; strong arms and legs that gave him a burly silhouette, made him look shorter than he was. He was a good tracker and hunter, knew little else. But, he liked money and he chased it as he had the beaver, the marten, the otter.

He had followed Jules up to Sky Valley from Santa Fe, thinking they might find gold or some way to make a good living. Jacques was not married and he had managed only to live off the land. He had nothing to fall back on, unlike Jules or Horne. Horne had his horse stock down on the flat, and Maria made things that could be sold for silver. He knew that Jules had a sister-in-law on the Arkansas and he thought he might do better down there, so he had left. Then the Utes had come and the people were in a panic. He had met Garcia and Delgado and they had told him there was money to be made if a man didn't care how he got it.

Jacques Berthoud was forty years old and he had nothing to show for it. Now, perhaps, he had a chance. Garcia's men lived well. In some ways, they reminded him of the free trappers he had known back in the thirties, not so much for their dispositions, but in the way they lived, lawless and free as the wind. There was a different form of camaraderie, he admitted, but at least he felt he belonged to a group. The Mexicans were professionals. They drank hard and played hard, but when it was time for business, they never flinched. He was still uneasy with Delgado, but Garcia was friendly enough and seemed to like him. He didn't trust Luis because the man hid himself so well. Berthoud could never tell what Delgado was thinking and that made him dangerous.

Like now. Where had he gone? And where was Reinhardt? They both should have been here to help with the pack animals. Even though Reinhardt was staying behind, Delgado was going back down the mountain.

"Mount your horse," said Garcia, jarring Berthoud from his reverie.

"Should we not wait for Luis?"

Garcia swung up into his saddle, settled between cantle and pommel. He pulled on his gloves, shook out his trousers. He wore a heavy buffalo coat, a scarf wrapped his head and ears underneath his rabbit felt hat.

"I told you, Pancho, he will catch up with us. Do not worry yourself about him."

Berthoud grunted, climbed into his saddle, the lead rope in his hand. He took up the slack and the mules inched forward. Garcia rode ahead, Jacques followed, bringing up the pack animals and their cargo. The air was sharp as a razor as they moved away from Reinhardt's cabin, the cold searching through Berthoud's sheepskin coat with gelid fingers.

He dreaded going back to the Pueblo, what was left of it. The horror was still etched on his mind, an indelible series of images that flickered on and off like candles in a wind. He, too, had seen the dead, but unlike Garcia and Delgado, he had seen the others, learned what had happened to Chepita following that grisly gray morning.

He and another man who lived in the village of St. Charles had learned, almost accidentally, the fate of Chepita. Tracking the Utes, Jacques and Ernesto Lopez found a wounded Jicarilla Apache up by a spring near Grape Creek, hiding in the brush. The Indian had crawled into the thicket to die. He spoke Spanish. Lopez put a pistol to the man's genitals and asked him about Chepita and the Sandoval boys.

"I die anyway," the Apache said.

"You'll die without eggs," said Lopez, cocking the hammer of the Colt's .36 caliber Navy. It had a brass frame, but it was pretty tight. He hadn't shot it much, but he meant what he said to the Jicarilla.

"The woman is dead already," said the Apache. "I was wounded when the Arapaho attacked us on Grape Creek. The Ute women all ran off into the woods. They took the captives with them. They took their lodges with them. After the fight, the Ute braves found their women and we all came up to this spring. The women were very sad because some good men had been killed. My brother was killed. One Arapaho shot me in the stomach. I took the arrow out, but I am passing blood and I am very weak."

"What about the Mexican woman and the two boys?" asked Jacques in broken Spanish.

Lopez asked it better in his native tongue.

"We stopped at this little spring and the Ute women were wailing and beating their breasts, tearing out their hair. This woman, Chepita, she was allowed to get off her pony and drink the water. She did this and then she bent down to wash her face. When she stood up, an arrow flew past her. She turned around and saw a Ute warrior standing by a tree. He had a bow and arrow in his hand and he was looking at her.

"This woman screamed and she started to run away. The Ute, I think his name is Little Bull, shot her in the back. The arrowhead came out through her breast. She grabbed the head of the arrow and pulled on it. She screamed and fell down. The children saw her fall and they picked up rocks and threw them at her until she died."

"What about the boys?" asked Lopez.

"The one called Felix asked why the children killed the woman. One of the Ute women, Clay Bowl, said that the Mexican woman was very sad and did not want to be comforted by them."

Lopez stood up and aimed his pistol at the Jicarilla's head. The Apache did not flinch when Lopez squeezed the trigger. The ball blew brains all over the tree behind the Apache's head. They left him there and followed the Ute tracks back to St. Charles. There, they learned that the Utes had just passed through. About two miles from Baca's house, they killed Marcelino's brother, Benito, and two Americans who had come from Bent's new fort in Big Timbers to buy corn from Baca.

The Indians stole forty head of cattle belonging to Levin Mitchell and killed a Pueblo Indian herder. They shot his Mexican companion in the back with arrows and rode on. The Mexican pretended to be dead, then staggered to St. Charles with three arrows sticking out of his back. Berthoud, Lopez and four other Americans chased the Utes, cornered them in a thicket beside the Arkansas River. They killed one and held siege for the rest of the day. Then, they went back to the village and the Utes escaped.

Jacques rode back to the Pueblo, where Garcia was waiting for him.

"It is time we went to see Dan Reinhardt," Garcia told him.

"About Horne?"

"Yes," said Garcia. "Horne has something we want."

"Horne will not be an easy man to get something from."

"He owes me, Pancho. I am just recalling a debt."

"I know," said Berthoud, and said no more. It was Garcia's business, not his. He was only a guide, he told himself. That was all. But, he thought of Horne then and he thought of him now. He didn't like Dan Reinhardt and Reinhardt had tried to kill Horne. The German had made a bad mistake. If Horne recovered from his wounds, the mistake might even be fatal. . . .

The horse jumped under Berthoud and he felt the slack go out of the lead rope as the mules balked. A shaved second later he heard the report. The rifle shot cracked, then reverberated in the valley, boomed off rock and echoed into an eerie silence.

"What was that?" asked Jacques. Garcia's horse, too, had spooked and he was reining hard as the animal twisted in a half-circle, tugging the leather straps right and left to bring his mount under control.

"None of our business," said Garcia.

Jacques felt something go cold inside him. He looked up at the lead-gray sky and the endless green spruce and pine and fir with their snowy mantles and he felt his throat constrict. He wanted to ride out of the valley quick and get away from that sound that still rang in his ears. He wanted to run and never stop running. He wanted never to come to this valley again.

Garcia calmed his horse and continued down the trail that led to the Poudre and the road to the flat. He looked back once and grinned at Berthoud.

Jacques felt a sickness boil in his stomach. He felt the terrible silence in the wake of the shot and he didn't want to think about it anymore.

The crack of the rifle. It had sounded so final. Just one shot. Not two or three. Just one.

Someone had died when that shot was fired.

Jacques knew who it must be and he felt like a traitor. At that moment, he almost wished that he had taken the bullet himself.

His ears still heard it. The rifle shot, echoing and echoing and echoing.

Forever.

•CHAPTER 10•

T HE WINTER RUSHED DOWN ON THE VALLEY ONCE
again, blowing in the cold north air, the
snow, keeping people close to their cabins,
locking the private secrets in even tighter. Horne's
arm and wrist healed quickly, for he was yet
strong and vital, and his flesh scarred over like
bark to the tree, leaving only memories and new
flesh that had pushed through the holes like taffy,
congealed into small patchworks of soft pink
lumps.

Before the storm hit there was only one thing
that happened out of the ordinary and Mary Lee
didn't make sense out of it at the time.

"Horne, did you take your snowshoes?" she
asked.

"Take 'em where?"

"Anywhere," she said. "They're gone."

"Maybe they fell off my horse when Jules
brought me back in."

"No. I put them away, out in the shed where you keep them."

"I keep them there in summer, not in winter."

"Where do you keep them in winter?"

He looked at her as if she was addled.

"Hanging just outside the door, or leaning up against the cabin."

"I greased them down, hung them in the shed," she said.

"Animal got 'em, I reckon. There's some likes to chew on the leather, the wood. You greased 'em, might make 'em more tasty to critters."

"Maybe," she said and dropped the subject. But, she hadn't seen any animal tracks out there, and now that she thought of it, there had been a lot of human tracks by the shed. The snow was all roiled up.

Horne forgot about it, and so did she. She first had noticed the snowshoes were missing just two days after Horne was shot, but now it seemed just another of those unsolved puzzles that was not worth bothering about when there were other things to tend to.

She went back to sleeping on the buffalo robe before the fire and watching Horne out of the corners of her eyes, wondering about him. She asked him once if he thought he ought to see a doctor. She had heard him talking in his sleep, crying out in pain.

"Man's either a fool or his own physician after he turns thirty," he told her. "I been hurt before, and I reckon I will again."

They did not have to wait long before something happened that was to disrupt their lives once again. Although the storm had long since passed, the snow was deep in the valley and the high country was impassable. Horne had done some trapping, but he tired easily, still, and he was silent much of the time, leaving Mary Lee to her own thoughts and devices. Sometimes he read from one of his Shakespeare books or the Bible, or worked on one of the elkskins with a scraper he had made out of an old knife and a chunk of antler. Mary Lee continued to work on something of her own whenever he was not about, and she kept this in the bottom of her sewing basket, out of sight. Once, Horne had almost caught her working on it, but she had hidden it under her skirt and she was sure he had not seen what it was.

In that February of 1855, a man appeared at Horne's door, half stove-in from the bitter cold of the winter-locked mountains. Horne stood there, looking at the man, and beyond him, at his horse. He recognized the horse.

"Who you be?" he asked.

"It's me, Horne. Dave."

"Dave? Sheppers? Godamighty, man. Come in by the fire and we'll start peeling you down to something recognizable."

Mary Lee watched the man enter the cabin and wondered who he was. She had never heard Horne mention his name. He was bent over from the cold, but when he stood up, he was tall and lean. When he took off his capote he was even leaner, and his face was shrouded in bristle, his eyes red-rimmed, his cheeks aflame with cold. He had soft blue eyes, a weak, receding chin, a shock of thin brown, flecked-with-gray hair. He shivered before the fire.

"Put on some coffee, Mary Lee," Horne said. "This is Dave Sheppers who feeds and tends to my horses down at LaPorte every winter."

"I never heard you say his name before," she said, a note of reproach in her voice.

"I better tend to Mollie," said Dave.

"I'll put her up. You get warm, son," Horne said.

He left the cabin without donning a coat and Mary Lee was left alone with the stranger. She was wise enough not to question him, though. She put water on to boil and ground up the coffee beans. The kitchen smelled faintly of cinnamon and fresh ground coffee. Dave Sheppers shook as he stood before the fire, rubbing his red hands together, squinting his eyes into little fists from the pain.

"Christ," he said once and moved away from the fire. His trousers were steaming.

Horne returned a few moments later, clomping in, leaving a trail of snow lumps across the polished floor. Mary Lee poured hot coffee into tin cups, set them on the table. Horne moved the table closer to the fire, set a chair for Sheppers.

"Set," he said, "and when your teeth stop being nervous, you can tell me why you made the ride."

"B-bad news, Jack," said Dave, holding the cup up to his face, washing his face in the steam.

"I reckoned it was. Couldn't it have waited till spring? You don't want to ride these mountains in the dead of winter just for a social call."

"Rustlers," said Sheppers and swilled the coffee into his mouth, swallowed. His Adam's apple, so sharp it looked like it would puncture his skin, moved up and down as his muscles contracted.

"Yeah?"

"Took some seventy head, including Champion and Coal."

Mary Lee stood away from the table, watching the two men. She saw a shadow cloud Horne's face and his eyes flicker with a dangerous light.

"Champ," he said softly. "And Coal, too. Damn." The two geldings were his pride and joy, high-stepping trotters with five gaits apiece, each horse sixteen and a half hands high. Champ was a sorrel; Coal was as black as his name, with a splotch of white blazed on the top of his forehead. Horne felt the swirl of sickness in his stomach, fought down the rising bile in his throat.

"You know 'em?" he asked.

"Mexes, right enough. Comancheros, maybe. I seen 'em before. They come up to LaPorte about a month or so ago. Pedro Garcia rides up front and Luis Delgado's his *segundo*."

"I know 'em, too," said Horne. "They got hot Yaqui blood in their veins."

"Mr. Horne, I'm real sorry."

"Dave. They kill anybody?"

Dave's head toppled forward. His shoulders drooped. He took off his hat, twisted the brim in thorny hands. Tears misted his eyes.

" 'Fraid so. Jimmy Hemphill got in Garcia's way. Pedro, he gunned the kid down. Warn't nothin' I could do about it. Delgado had me at the business end of a rifle."

"Christ," swore Horne. "Jimmy wasn't but, what? Nineteen?"

"Twenty and some," said Sheppers, biting his lip. His hat was twisted out of shape like a washrag.

"Just two of 'em? For seventy head?"

"They was three," said Sheppers. "Other one, well, he's one you know, too. The Frenchie, Berthoud."

"Jacques Berthoud? He was riding with Garcia?"

"I reckon so. He didn't look like he cottoned to it, none, but he damn sure wrangled them horses out of the corrals."

"That goddamned Pedro," said Horne, looking off into the fire.

"You know him, eh?"

"Once or twice we met up," reflected Horne. "We had a run-in down in Socorro some time back. I knew him in Santa Fe before that."

"That Socorro business," said Sheppers. "Didn't I hear about that?"

"Pedro must carry some weighty grudge," said Horne. "Jimmy was with me that time. We brought up wild ones we caught up on the Gila and Garcia took offense. He thought those horses were his personal property."

"Hell, a man wouldn't carry a grudge over a few head of wild horses. I recollect you and Jimmy only brought up about a dozen head or so."

"There was some shooting. I killed Pedro's little brother, Felix."

Sheppers let out a low whistle.

Mary Lee stood quiet, watching Horne intently. She searched his face, her gaze lingering on his shadowy eyes, the features etched hard by the orange flames in the hearth. She held her breath as if afraid she would be noticed, as if fearful of being sent away.

Horne didn't tell Sheppers the rest of it. He felt Mary Lee's gaze on him, kept his face a mask. There was no use in bringing up that other business. The Socorro thing was bad enough. Pedro had sent his best guns against him, including Felix, and Horne took them down. But, there was another time when he and Garcia had a conflict of interest. That was over a woman, Perla Luz, in Santa Fe. Garcia was in love with Perla, but she could not bear his cruelty. She gave her love to Horne and when Garcia found out about it, he tried once again to kill Horne. Horne beat him half to death with his bare fists. Garcia vowed then to make Horne pay. His first act had been to kill Perla while Horne was driving a string of horses up to Cherry Creek. Horne had not seen Garcia since, though he had ridden up and down the Gila and stopped at all the places where the Mexican had ever tied a horse to a hitchrail.

"I can see where the man might want to get back at you," said Sheppers. "Killin' his brother like you did."

"Yeah," said Horne. "I guess that's it."

Sheppers looked over at the girl. He drank the rest of his coffee, held out his cup.

"You get yourself hitched?" he asked Horne.

"No," said Horne, rising from the table. He stalked to the other end of the cabin, took his gunbelt down from the buffalo horn rack, threw it on the bed. He lifted the Hawken and rubbed the barrel with his sleeve.

"You fixin' to go after Garcia?" asked Sheppers. "He headed south."

"I know where he went," said Horne. "I been hearin' about him and his bunch down at the Pueblo."

"The Utes killed pert' near ever'one down at the Pueblo," said Sheppers. "Man came up six weeks ago wantin' to buy some horses. He didn't have the price."

"Utes?" asked Horne.

"That's what he said. Went on a rampage. Army's out huntin' 'em now."

"That's a hell of a note," said Horne, carrying the rifle to the table. He lifted it to his shoulder several times. His left arm still had kinks in it. His wrist was weaker than it had been, but he could use it. "You rest up a couple of days, Dave. Then we'll go on down to LaPorte. How long it take you to ride up?"

"Four days," said Sheppers.

"We'll make it in two," said Horne.

Sheppers kept looking at the girl as he drank the rest of his coffee. She had her back to him, but he had already seen the looks she gave Horne.

He had also seen that Horne hardly noticed her. He wondered about that. It was mighty strange, he thought. Horne living with a woman like that. She was young and pretty and obviously stuck on Horne.

"Jack," he said the next morning, when Horne awakened him in the tack room where he had slept, "what about the girl?"

"What about her?"

"She belong to you?"

"No. She doesn't belong to anybody."

"Well, it ain't none of my business, but. . . ."

"That's right, Dave," interrupted Horne, "it's none of your business."

· CHAPTER 11 ·

HORNE TRIED TO IGNORE MARY LEE AS HE MADE preparations to go down the mountain and take up the trail after Garcia. She stayed out of his way as he measured out grain for the trail, packed jerky and made hardtack, cleaned his guns and filled his powder horn, set out caps and extra ball and powder.

"I'll take all the stock down with me," he told her, while Dave was out tending to his horse. "You'd best go over to your folks and make peace with them. I thank you for taking care of me when I was laid up."

She opened her mouth to speak, but no sound came out. Instead, tears flooded her eyes and she ran off to the spring house where Horne kept his meat. It was really a kind of root cellar dug into a bank. He heard the door slam and knew she was sitting there on one of the salt barrels in the dark.

"Damned hard-headed woman," he muttered

and began to slam his gear around. The subject, he knew, would come up again before he rode off the mountain.

Dave Sheppers awoke in the darkness of the tack room, shivered in the chill. The fire in the iron woodstove had burned down, but when he opened the door, he saw the coals glittering like orange jewels beneath the ashes. He poked kindling wood into the ashes, laid the sticks over the coals and closed the door. The wood caught and he fed the flames with short logs until the heat began to soak through him.

The room smelled of leather and linament, of salve and salt, of damp wool and grain, but it was built tight and Sheppers was grateful for the warmth. He was still not thawed out from his ride up the mountain. Last night, he wondered if he would ever be warm again. The high country was not to his liking, never had been. He liked horses, though, and tall grass and wide meadows. Horne raised the best horses he had ever tended, and Dave had worked ranches from the Red River to the Rio Grande. Born in New Orleans, in 1816, he had gone to Texas like so many others and found the vastness of the sky and the land to be more compelling than the gambling halls and brothels of New Orleans. He had drifted ever westward, following the Arkansas, finally, to the Platte and running into Horne one day at an auction, admiring the horseflesh he had brought down from the high mountain meadows. They had become friends and Dave had tended his horses during the winter for the past six or seven years.

Dave raised his own stock, good Missouri trotters that he sold to eastern sportsmen and Tennessee stock that he sold to the army. He had never married, but he courted a girl from LaPorte and had been thinking lately of asking her to be his wife. When Garcia raided him, his own horses had been out to pasture, so he had lost no stock. Yet, he felt responsible for Horne's loss, and he knew Horne would want to know before spring. He had not been to Horne's place in winter before and he wondered how the man could stand the cold. The ride up had been hell, with the wind roaring down the Poudre canyon, slashing at his face, burning into his bones until they ached. He shuddered now to think of having to do it all over again. The only consolation was that he would be riding down, not up, and at the end of the trail there would be a warm fire and protection against the knifing wind.

Horne banged on the door of the tack room.

"Dave, you up?"

"Just. Come on in."

Dave stood there in his long underwear as Horne ducked his head and entered the dark room.

"I'm packing up," said Horne.

"It's still dark out."

"I know the way."

"I'd like to get some vittles in me."

"You go on in. Mary Lee will burn some venison for you, I reckon. There's beans and hot coffee."

"You eat already?"

"I don't break my fast the mornings I hunt," said Horne, grabbing a saddle off a sawhorse, hefting it in his big arms. Horne stalked out of the room and kicked the door shut.

Dave shivered at the blast of cold air that blew in with the smell of horse apples and ammonia from the corral.

Horne came inside the cabin after Dave had finished his breakfast. Mary Lee was wiping the skillet dry with a hand-mop she had made from a piece of sheepskin.

"I want to go with you, Horne," she said softly.

"Why?"

"I just want to be with you. Maybe you're not as well as you think you are. You still got a knot on your head the size of a darning egg and. . . ."

"You ought to be back with your kin."

"No. Don't you understand? I can't ever go back there. I won't go back there."

"Won't, can't, no matter," he said. "You ain't goin' with me."

"I will, Jackson Horne," she said, and he saw the look of defiance on her face, the glint of determination in her eyes, the upward tilt of her chin.

"No, you won't, girl, and that's that. You ask me, you need a good strapping."

"You wouldn't dare," she spat.

"Don't tempt me," he said.

Horne belted his Spanish pistols, gathered up his Hawken, possibles pouch, horn, and the extra powder, ball and percussion caps, stalked out of the cabin. Dave was playing push-pull with one of the mules, Gideon, trying to get him and the lead rope together. The sun was just smearing the sky a pale rouge to the east and the wind had dropped off to a low keen in the trees, barely noticeable. Horne sheathed the Hawken in its tough cowhide boot and hung his possibles pouch from the saddle horn. Dancer didn't move as Horne stuffed the extra ammunition in one of his saddle bags.

"Gideon, you sonofabitch," Horne said and jerked the animal's halter rope. Gideon got into line and Dave ran the lead rope through the D-rings, hooking all the mules together. The packs were all covered with buffalo robes that could be used as shelter on the trip, and they were tied securely with diamond hitches. Horne checked all the panniers and the hitches, went back inside the cabin for his bedroll and grub.

Mary Lee passed him at the door, carrying a sack over her shoulder. He watched as she went out to the corral, whistled for her pony.

"Looks like she figures to foller us," said Dave.

Horne went inside the cabin, slammed the door. When he emerged a few moments later with his grubsack and a poncho, he saw that Mary Lee had her pony under saddle, was loading meat from the spring house into her saddlebags. He heard the clank of a skillet.

Horne packed the grubsack and tied the poncho atop his bedroll. He walked back to the cabin and made a last check of the fire, saw that all the windows were battened down. He wouldn't lock the cabin. A hungry man, or a cold one, might have need of a warm place and food while he was gone. Others in the valley, he noted, were not so tolerant. These, usually, were the biggest thieves, so keen on protecting their own goods, they had little regard for the possessions of others.

"Goodbye, Mary Lee," Horne called.

"I'm going with you, Horne," she yelled back.

"You go on home," he said, and nodded to Sheppers.

"Stubborn, ain't she?" David grinned.

"Let's get moving," gruffed Horne.

Sheppers mounted up, pulled on the lead rope. The mules and horses plodded forward, the packs swaying under the buffalo robes. Horne took the lead, but not before Sheppers noticed the look on his face, the cold glint in his eyes.

Horne turned back twice before they reached the main trail along the Poudre. Mary Lee was following them, sure enough, and he chased her away.

"Fool girl," he shouted. "You'd best go back before it's too late."

Mary Lee never answered. Finally, Horne just kept going, setting a pace that was not good for the animals as they trudged up to the top of the ridge that rimmed the lower end of the valley. There, he looked back, but didn't see the woman.

He knew, however, that she was still following them. He knew it in his heart, damn her, and he didn't know what to do about it.

"Mr. Horne," Sheppers said, at the top of the ridge, "we'd best lay up so's the critters and me can catch our breaths."

"She's back there, Dave, damnitall."

"Well, she's liable to be the one to bury us if we don't slow down some."

Horne knew Sheppers was right. He sighed, rocked back against his cantle, cocked a leg around the saddlehorn. Sheppers built a smoke and they waited in the snow-flocked timber for the girl to catch up with them. A half hour later, she hadn't showed.

"Maybe she turned back," said Sheppers.

"Maybe the Poudre runs with blackstrap molasses," Horne replied.

They rode down the other side of the ridge. The trail widened there and Sheppers's tracks coming up were still visible. There were wolf and mule deer tracks crossing the trail, and Horne saw a white-furred mink nab a cutthroat trout from the edge of the Poudre. The animal lifted its head regally and watched him pass with eyes shining like obsidian beads.

Horne spelled Sheppers with the mules and horses, let Dave take the lead. He kept looking back over his shoulder, but by late afternoon he had not seen Mary Lee again and hoped that she had finally listened to reason and turned back.

"We'll camp where the Poudre runs through the moraine," Horne told Sheppers. It was a favorite spot, with plenty of timber and firewood, a wide expanse that no one could cross easily. Eons ago, perhaps, an avalanche had roared through this part of the mountains leaving boulders strewn in its wake. It looked as if someone had taken a giant sledge and hammered every stone, cracking them like walnuts just for the sheer joy of it.

The spot Horne chose offered a maximum of protection, a view in all directions. He showed Sheppers where to picket the pack animals and the horses. The snow was not so deep in the shelter of the timber and the wind had blown much of it away, so there was dry fodder if they wanted to work for it. Horne made camp as the sun hung on the craggy peaks like a shimmering coin.

He built a fire and laid out his bedroll. Dave laid his gear on the other side of the fire and the two men set to fixing supper before the wind began to roam down the canyon, sniffing like a wolf on the prowl. The horses whickered and Horne looked up from the skillet to see Mary Lee crossing the moraine, her pony picking its way carefully across the jumble of boulders.

Sheppers grinned.

"Shut up," said Horne softly.

He didn't say a word when Mary Lee rode up. He watched as she stripped her pony, hobbled it in a grove of aspen. She unpacked her saddlebags, laid out her bedroll a couple of feet from Horne's.

"I brought candles," she said, "in case you forgot."

Horne said nothing.

"That's good, Miss Simmons," said Sheppers and Horne wanted to throttle him.

They ate beans and elk for supper. Mary Lee and Dave chattered away like a pair of magpies while Horne savaged his food like a bear with its snout in a grease bucket. He made so much noise the other two had to raise their voices to be heard.

"You must have left your manners back at the cabin," she told Horne, as she daintily dabbed at her mouth with a cloth she had brought along as a serviette.

"You must have left your brains back there," he growled, scowling at her. He got up from the fire, threw his leavings out some distance from camp and did not return for the better part of an hour.

Mary Lee was snugged down for the night in her bedroll. Dave was attaching a bell to Gideon's halter. The sky was clear and the stars looked like spilled diamonds, so close and big in the thin air that they seemed only a few miles away. The moon was not yet up and the darkness was broken only by the shimmering ribbon of light thrown off by the Poudre two hundred yards away, the orange glow of the campfire.

"I'll take the first watch," said Horne.

"You think we need to keep a lookout?"

"You never know."

"Maybe because of the girl."

"Dave, you know, sometimes you talk too damned much."

"Hell, there ain't nobody within thirty miles of us. . . ."

"I know—you think too damned much. Get some sleep. I'll wake you in a few hours."

"Well, that girl is plumb stuck on you and you can't brush her away like a blow-fly."

"That's my worry."

"It sure as hell is," said Dave and stomped away, leaving Horne alone in the darkness with Gideon. The mule shook its head and the brassy clank of the bell made an alien, lonesome sound in the stillness.

The wind stirred and the chill floated down off the high peaks and made the fire flutter as it passed, roaming, roaming through the night like an exodus of ghosts.

Horne pulled his coat tight about him and pulled his rifle out of its scabbard.

"Good night, Horne," said Mary Lee as he passed close to her.

He almost answered her.

• CHAPTER 12 •

WHEN SHEPPERS CAME TO WAKE UP HORNE IN the morning, he noticed Mary Lee had rolled over in her bedroll until she was snuggled up against Horne, frontways to his back.

They fit together like a pair of spoons, he thought, rubbing his eyes. He was sleepy, cold, as he stirred the fire. He prodded Horne with the butt of his rifle, saw the man's bedroll move. Horne poked his head outside into the still, cold air. It was still dark, but the stars were fading in a paling sky. Dawn was poised somewhere down canyon and the wind had died to a faint whisper, leaving only a chill ash in its wake.

"Mornin', Horne."

Horne massaged the knot on his head. He had banged it during the night and it throbbed like a gouty toe in the frosty air.

"All quiet?" he asked.

"Nary a Injun or catamount come by."

Horne fixed Sheppers with a look.

"You've got mouth, Dave, I'll give you that."

Sheppers grinned. But he stepped back as Horne looked around for something handy to throw.

Horne pulled his boots out from the bottom of his bedroll, slipped his stockinged feet inside before they had a chance to cool. Dave stirred the fire, added kindling until it blazed up, then put aspen logs on to build up the heat. By the time Horne returned from the river, Mary Lee was up, had the coffee on. The aroma hit Horne just about the time the sun poked through the bottom of the canyon, spilling a buttery hue over the rocks of the moraine and making the Poudre dance with silver sparks.

"We'll have coffee and then pack up and be on our way," said Horne.

"No breakfast?" chided Mary Lee.

"We got hardtack if we need something in our bellies," said Horne, "and just enough for two."

"Just enough for two," she mocked.

Sheppers suppressed a smile. Horne fixed him with a withering glare.

"You'll drink my coffee, though, won't you?" Mary Lee persisted.

"It's my coffee," said Horne, grabbing a porcelainized tin cup from his saddlebag, "you just boiled it."

Mary Lee nodded in silent agreement. Dave frowned. He kicked a log end to push it back into the fire and dug in his sack for a coffee cup.

Horne drank quickly, wiped out his cup with snow and packed it away. He went after his horse, brought him back to camp and threw the blanket on his back.

"You just as well go on back, girl," Horne said, as he threw on his saddle, "because you're just going to get left behind by and by."

"My name is Mary Lee," she said, "and I'm go-

ing wherever you go. The only way you can stop
me is to shoot me."

"I just might damned well do that," said Horne.

Horne and Sheppers never saw Mary Lee during
the day, but each night she would lay out her bedroll next to Horne's, and by morning, she was
snugged up next to him for warmth. She made no
other demands. Horne tried to appear calm and
collected, but Sheppers was a nervous wreck by
the time they rode out of the canyon and into the
little village of LaPorte—just ahead of a snow-
storm that soon dusted the foothills, closed the
high passes once again.

Mary Lee showed up later that day, shivering,
her teeth chattering like hailstones on a tin roof.
Her lips were blue from the cold and her eyes
sandpapered raw by the wind.

"Why won't she leave me be?" Horned muttered to himself.

"She looks plumb stove in," said Sheppers.

"Yeah."

"You worry about her, don't you?"

"I worry about all dumb creatures now and
again," said Horne.

Sheppers wisely did not comment.

She followed them to the ranch, nestled in a
wide valley in view of the foothills. The Poudre,
now part of the South Platte, ran through the middle of it—a slate gray on that cloudy, freezing day.
The main house sat on a low hill, presenting a
commanding view of the rolling countryside. The
corrals were strangely silent as the trio rode past
the log home to the stock pens. The bunkhouse
stood forlorn against the skyline. Horne winced
when he passed by it.

"That where Jimmy bunked?" he asked.

"That one yonder," said Dave. "It's got two rooms,

Jimmy slept in one of them." Horne looked beyond the bunkhouse, saw the small log cabin, its chimney smokeless, its windows boarded up tight.

"You show me when we get done," said Horne.

"Yeah," said Dave softly. "He got shot just outside the door."

"There'll be hell to pay."

"You got me backin' you, Horne."

"This is as far as you go, Dave. I'll go on by myself from here."

"But I . . ."

"I figure Garcia will have scouts watching his backtrail. He wants me to follow him, likely. He knows I'll come after him. Anybody else, he'll just shoot and be done with it."

"I don't know what you mean. Why won't he just shoot you?"

"He'll want me to die slow, I reckon."

"I'm not afraid to go."

"No, I know you're not, Dave. I'll need you here to take care of the stock."

"I got a boy can come over and do that."

"You stay here, Dave." Horne rode Tony up to the corral gate, dismounted. He was leading Dancer; Dave led the mules and other horses.

"Jesus, Horne," said Dave, swinging down from the saddle. "What about the girl?"

Horne loosened the belly cinch on Tony, pulled the saddle from his back.

"She's staying here."

"If you ask me," Sheppers began, "I'd say that gal has a powerful case of the . . ."

"I didn't ask you, Dave," interrupted Horne.

Mary Lee unsaddled her pony on the other side of the corral, well away from the men. She watched as Sheppers and Horne finished putting up the horses and mules, then turned her mount in with the others. Horne and the rancher walked off to the little house beyond the bunkhouse. Mary Lee added some extra grain to her pony's feed, waited while he ate it so the other horses would not horn in and take his portion.

She breathed a sigh when the men disappeared behind the bunkhouse. She patted the pony's withers, looked at the Arapaho love bracelet on her wrist. It no longer reminded her so strongly of Red Hawk, but it had become a token of both her slavery and her freedom, especially of her rescue. It held another meaning for her, as well. As it had bonded her to Red Hawk, now she hoped it would bond her to Horne. If only Horne could see how she felt about him, that she wanted to be with him always and could not bear to be away from him. She slid the beaded leather band back inside her sleeve quickly, stepped through the poles of the corral, picked up her saddlebags and bedroll, walked toward the house.

The back door was unlocked. A jiggle of the latch opened it. Mary Lee stepped into the musty back room, adjusted her eyes to the dim light. It was a small room, with a hallway leading to the kitchen. Bridles and halters, spurs and harness hung on wooden pegs set into the walls. Saddles and blankets lay along the walls and an open toolbox gleamed with implements: pliers, tongs, nail-pullers, a shoeing hammer, various knives, and tacks, nails, strips of leather, all in a jumble. She stepped through the hallway and into the kitchen.

The kitchen was small, too, but it was neat, with a small cookstove, pots and pans, ladles and spoons pegged to the walls. She saw a set of butcher and boning knives hanging over the counter. The room was cold and lifeless, but she saw the kindling and firewood stacked next to the stove. She put down her saddlebags and set to work. She banged cupboards, looked in the flour and sugar bins, found the potatoes and beans, some wild onions; a haunch of smoked beef hung in a little alcove beyond the stove. She found salt pork and slab bacon in a box that showed the gnawed grooves where rats had tried to eat through the wood.

She put kindling in the firebox and lit the dry sticks before she went through the rest of the house, curious about a place where Horne sometimes hung his hat. There were two bedrooms, a front room with heavy chairs and a divan, some tables, rifles on the walls, a fireplace, and dust thick as fur on a beaver everywhere she looked.

Somehow, the room made her feel closer to Horne, as if she had just opened another closet and found some of his clothes hanging there. But it was cold and musty in the room, and smelled of woodsmoke and tobacco, sweat and the faint, lingering tang of whiskey. The fireplace was laid, and she lit a taper, started the fire to take the chill out of the room. Smoke billowed in the chimney before the draft caught it and pulled it up the flue.

She looked into the bedrooms. One was Sheppers's, obviously, with the bed rumpled and unmade, and the other was neatly vacant—the walls decorated with Indian artifacts, the bed made tight, the wool blanket taut as a drumhead on the mattress.

Horne's room, she thought, and her heart beat wildly in her chest. The house creaked as the heat from the two sources warmed it and Mary Lee withdrew from Horne's bedroom, reluctantly, fighting down her curiosity with an effort of will. She wanted to look into the wardrobe, search the bureau for more clues to his other life, his past.

For Horne, she realized, was still as big a mystery now as when she had first fallen in love with him.

She had hated him, at first, hated him for killing Red Hawk and for bringing her back to Sky Valley.

But she had already learned before he came for her that hate could turn to love.

She had hated Red Hawk, yet, as time went by, he had unlocked something strange and powerful inside her—not with his violence, but with his magnetism, the brilliant hardness somewhere at his core that drew her to him like a magnet draws an iron filing to its cold surface.

Horne had that same mystery to him, but he was different. He had not ravaged her, although he'd had many opportunities, but he had proved stronger than Red Hawk. And, without his knowing or trying, he had become her captor. She was as much his prisoner as she had been Red Hawk's, perhaps even more so.

Yet Horne did not know about the feelings that boiled within her, the terrible confusion she felt whenever he was near, the heat she felt whenever she touched him while he slept. Her feeling for him was a kind of torture. And she was frightened by the idea that the love she had for Horne could turn back again so easily to hate.

Hate. She didn't understand it any more than she did love. But the two emotions were intertwined—walked in violent lockstep through the tangles of her feelings—ready to explode at any moment, burst her heart asunder and leave her broken and lifeless, empty and dead.

The tears came unbidden as she stoked the firebox and laid in a log. Smoke seeped through the iron lids and along the welded seams of the stove, tiny spiraling wisps that sought a draft, an escape into the outside world.

"Oh Horne," she sobbed, "damn you, damn you, damn you!"

•CHAPTER 13•

HORNE STOOD THERE AS SHEPPERS OPENED THE door.

"This was where Jimmy bunked," said Dave, unable to look at the bed. His voice sounded as if someone had poured sand down his throat. "I'll leave you to look around. He—he was killed ju—just outside."

"I know," said Horne. He had seen the dried smears on the wood, looking like rust, like raw red wounds—fingerprints on a man's throat—scars that would never go away no matter how hard a man scrubbed at them. He would look at the stains again, when he had his wits in order, when he could swallow normal again.

Dave bowed sheepishly and walked away toward the house. Horne went inside, after a moment, steeling himself against the memories he knew would come flooding in on him. He had liked Jimmy Hemphill a lot and could still remember

Jimmy's bright smile, his quick eyes, sparkly as sunlight glancing off quartz or mica chips in a summer stream. Jimmy was from Texas and wild as a tumbleweed when he first came to Colorado on a trail drive. He loved horses, loved to break them—gentle if he could, with a hardwood post or a quirt if he couldn't.

Horne remembered that first wild horse he had given to Jimmy. It was a roman-nosed buckskin with fire in its eyes, smoke jetting out of its nostrils like a dragon. Horne had halter-broken him, but the animal had never had a saddle on his bowed back until that raw spring day when Jimmy climbed aboard. It was a mean trick to play on a kid, maybe, but Horne wanted to see if the young buck had sand and there wasn't much time, with sixty head to break and a man up at Fort Laramie waiting for them, cash in hand.

When that hardhead horse started bucking, Horne watched Jimmy to see how he would handle it. The buckskin looked at the kid, rolled its eyes into a stare like the devil had hold of its windpipe and started to grow a hump along its backbone before the lad touched a boot-toe to the stirrup. For just a second, Horne started to call it off, get the kid back to the fence rail. The mustang had a killer look in its eye and its hooves were poised like hammers ready to claw flesh off Jimmy's bones and smash the kid to a green pulp in a pile of horse apples. But Horne held back and Jimmy jerked the horse's blunt-nosed head down and put him to chasing his tail while he climbed aboard. He did it quick, as if he was mounting a gentle dobbin, and then he let up on the reins as he clamped his legs around the horse's middle like a pair of parentheses. The buckskin jumped straight up, his back bowed like a rainbow, his ears laid back flat as a terrier's, and scratched at the nearest cloud, the sonofabitch. There was little sky showing between Jimmy's butt and the saddle. The horse fishtailed, clawed, bent double into the shape of a horseshoe, chased its tail, did everything it could to throw the man, but Jimmy stuck to it like he had flypaper on his seat. He rode the horse down, broke its spirit, made it docile as a lamb. Jimmy had the horse eating out of his hand, licking the salt-sweat off his palm as if they had growed up together like weeds in a pepper patch.

Sadness washed over Horne as he remembered that shining day and now looked around the room where Jimmy had spent his last days on earth. It was a painful moment for Horne as he looked at the empty boots under the bunk, saw a shirt hanging on a nail, a crumpled pair of trousers on the seat of a chair. He choked up, quelled his anger. The kid's pistol lay on the table, holstered, the belt curled around it, useless as a teat on a boar. A Navy .44, grip like a plowhandle, sleek as sculpture, with its fluted barrel stamped with Sam Colt's name in solid steel.

"Goodbye, Jimmy," croaked Horne, and he staggered outside to look again at the dull, autumn-hued blaze of blood on the log walls of the cabin. This was where the kid had lost his life. Horne could almost feel the boy's pain and sorrow at life being wrested from him against his will. The ground seemed to drop out from under Horne and he closed his eyes, trying to blot out the image of the boy taking the bullets into his flesh, slipping down into the dirt, brilliant freshets of blood streaming from his wounds.

He stalked toward the house, numb with his hatred for the men who had done this to Jimmy.

The horses the three men had stolen did not make any difference. He didn't care about them anymore. But Jimmy, he had to count for something. His smile was worth ten of Delgado, thirty of Garcia and a hundred of that traitorous Frenchman, Berthoud. His death had to be paid for. Paid for dearly and in kind.

Horne sat at the table and ate, feeding his face like a man on the way to the gallows, but he said nothing during the meal, although Mary Lee and Dave tried to draw him out. He answered in heboar grunts until they left him alone, and the silence grew long in the kitchen, broken only by the click of utensils against tin plates and the soft mindless munch of teeth on food that had gone tasteless as rain-wet sawdust.

"I thank you for the meal," said Horne as he arose from the table and started toward the door. "When you finish up, Dave, I'll see you in the bunkhouse."

"You're welcome," said Mary Lee as he left. She was stunned for a moment by his abrupt departure. "What's the matter with him?" she asked Dave.

"It's that kid, Jimmy. They were pretty close."

"I never heard him mention him."

"Horne don't never talk much. Not about—some things."

"I know," she mused, looking beyond Dave into the abstraction of the wall with its still-lifes of ladles and iron pots. "But, he seems different, almost a different man. Now, I mean."

"He's probably thinkin' 'bout them Mexicans."

"You mean his horses."

"Oh, I think he means to get his horses back, but I seen him when he come back from lookin' at Jimmy's stuff. He means to kill a man or my name ain't David Sheppers."

Mary Lee shuddered. She had seen Horne like

that before. She knew Dave was right. There was a look about Horne that made the skin on her arm ripple with goosebumps.

"Why? He can't bring Jimmy back," she said, half to herself.

"Horne's thataway. He don't say much, maybe, but he moves when he wants to get to a place, do a thing. I asked him once why he took on all this horse business when he could just roam the land and live free like he always has."

"And what did he tell you?"

"He said it was a mite better to run with the hounds for your dinner than with the rabbit for your life."

Dave swabbed his plate with a cornmeal biscuit, heavy as a chunk of galena, sopping up gravy from the stew Mary Lee had made.

"I was going to say that Horne couldn't go up against those Mexicans alone," she said, "but I knew that wouldn't be true."

"What do you mean?"

"He went up against a whole tribe of Arapaho by himself," she said, sighing deeply.

"He never spoke a word of it. I knew he was gone a long time and when he come back, he said he had been hunting Injuns."

"That's all he said?"

"Yes, ma'am."

"He is a strange man, isn't he, Dave?"

"I don't know. He reminds me of my pa. Maybe that's why I like him so much. My pa never said much, either, but when he come into a room, he made the sparks fly off the wheel. And when he spoke, he made you feel like he had waited a long time to tell you something real important."

Mary Lee laughed.

"I know what you mean," she said. "My pa isn't

110

like that. But, Horne, well, he says more by not saying than most people do giving a speech."

"You got that right, Miss. I better get on out there and see what he wants. You fix a mighty fine supper, Mary Lee."

"Why, thank you, David. I hope you know I wish we could become friends. I'm going with Horne. Wherever he goes."

"Yes'm," he said, but he turned away from her and stood up.

She watched him put on his hat and leave and listened to the kitchen tick with silence after he left.

Horne had a lamp burning in the bunkhouse. Dave stepped inside, closed the door. It was clear outside, and cold. He had broken ice on the pond that afternoon and he knew it would freeze over again by morning. Horne stood by the table in the center of the room, one boot up on a chair he gripped with his left hand.

"What's on your mind, Jack?" asked Sheppers.

"A couple of things, Dave. Set."

"No, I'm tired of settin'. Three days of saddle and another at supper."

Horne laughed.

"All right." He moved his left arm under his coatsleeve, testing the muscles, the tendons. "I got a funny feeling, like I've left my back door open."

"I don't foller you, Horne."

"Garcia went on up to Sky Valley, then he come here and shot Jimmy Hemphill, stole my horses. Has Reinhardt ever been here?"

"Big feller. I remember him. Long time back. Late summer. He looked at your stock, didn't buy anything."

"That's what I figured."

"You think he put Garcia up to takin' your horses?"

"The more I think about it, he might have been the man who bushwhacked me. He's big enough to make the tracks I saw. Maybe I should have put it to him before I come down here."

"Maybe. He ever talk to you about buying a horse?"

"No," said Horne.

"Funny, he said he'd deal with you when he was here. I paid it no mind at the time."

"Well, nothing I can do about it now. It's just something to keep in mind."

"What else?" asked Dave.

"That gal in there." Horne sat down at the table where the hands played cards on summer evenings or sat and darned their socks while they swapped lies.

"She's got her mind set on follerin' you to hell."

"I don't want her on my tail when I head south, Dave. I mean it."

"How you gonna stop her?"

"You keep her here. Any way you can. If you have to tie her up—lock her in this bunkhouse."

"I can't do that, Horne."

"You'd better, Dave. I'm going to leave tonight, while she's asleep. I want that Gideon mule packed with grub and camp gear, ammunition. I'll take Tony, he's better for the long ride, and Stepper to spell him. I expect I'll wear one or the other out before I come back."

"What time you gonna leave?"

"Just after midnight. When Mary Lee is bedded down tight, I'll just sneak out quiet. I want everything ready, my horse saddled, my Hawken in its boot."

"She thinks a heap of you, Jackson."

"I think a lot of her, too. That's why she's not

going to dog my trail. Garcia wouldn't think twice about putting a ball in her. Him or Delgado. I can't say about the Frenchman."

"I can't figure that Frenchie out. Thought he was an old friend of yours."

"Berthoud never was a friend. He trapped with one of the brigades." Horne stood up, felt the beard on his face.

"I'll have everything set for you, Horne. I don't know how long I can keep her here, though. She's pigheaded as a sow in a turnip patch."

"Just don't tell her where I'm headed. She'll get over it and go back home."

"I don't think she'll ever go back home," said Dave. "I think you're the only home she wants."

"Dave, that girl has been bullboated between the rocks. She and her sisters kidnapped and raped by a bunch of Arapaho bucks, the sisters murdered, her pa clubbed into a senseless cabbage-head. She walks in circles right now, but she'll come to her senses. Right now she's more Injun than white. I think she took to the ways of the Arapaho while she was with 'em. She needs to get back with her people, get some solid ground under her high-tops."

"Why don't you want her?" Dave asked, point-blank.

Horne picked at a splinter of wood in the table, gouging it with his thumb. He flexed the muscles in his left wrist, working out the stiffness. His shoulder twitched with a sudden twinge of dull pain. The soreness was still there, reminding him of the ball that had struck him. The simple questions were sometimes the hardest to answer. He looked up at Sheppers. Dave's eyes were in shadow. Light grazed his chin, the faint beard that had begun to grow on the trail from Sky Valley.

"A man has his ways," said Horne. "I got mine,

same as any. Set long before Mary Lee came
bustin' in on me. She's a fair and comely woman,
I reckon, and good enough for any man lookin' for
female company. If you believe in luck, I've not
had much with the women. Two of 'em have died.
Murdered. That sticks in my craw. Pretty fine
women. Maybe I want better for this one."

"You care for her, then."

"I care for her," said Horne.

• CHAPTER 14 •

THE MEN BEGAN TO GATHER AT MCGONIGLE'S. LOUIS
Simmons had sent Chollie's son Gary to
summon them to the trading post. Chollie
stood on the porch, barely recognizable in his
thick buffalo coat and cap with its wide earflaps.

"What's in the hopper, Chollie?" asked Berle
Campbell as he tied his horse to the hitchrail.

"We got trouble, Berle. Big trouble. Go on inside."

Bill McPherson came, and Faron MacGregor,
and the last, a man named Peter Stewart, who was
a nephew of McPherson married to Luke Newcastle's widow, Charity. Chollie followed him inside,
closed the door to the light snowfall blowing a
floury dust over the porch.

Louis Simmons stood next to the stove, talking
to Dan Reinhardt, his face hardened to a mask of
outrage. As always, he tugged at his scraggle-
beard, smoothed the horseshoe of his moustache

115

that framed his small mouth. His paunch billowed out his macintosh coat, strained the buttons. Dan held a lone snowshoe in his hand.

"What the hell's this all about?" bellowed McPherson, his temper, as always, short-fused, hair-triggered. His pinched face seemed scoured to a dangerous redness as the cords of his neck-muscles swelled.

"Murder, that's what it's about," said Simmons. "Murder most foul, Bill McPherson. Right on our doorstep. Right under our noses."

"Aye, calm yoursel'," said Faron, "and tell us who's been murdered and who ha' done the deed."

"Chollie found 'em," raged Lou Simmons, "found 'em slaughtered like sheep, and by God, we know who did it."

"Chollie?" asked McPherson.

Chollie, a bearish man with tangled blond hair, walked over to the circle of men and shook his head sadly.

"Jules Moreaux was shot between the eyes," he told them. "His wife, Maria, was strangled. They're both dead."

There was a collective gasp as the men in the room who had not heard the news recoiled in shock. Questions boiled up in a tangle of conversation that couldn't be sorted out until there was silence.

"Listen, listen," shouted Simmons to quiet the men down. "Listen to Chollie. He found 'em, and Dan here has one of Horne's snowshoes."

"What happened?" asked McPherson, his eyes flashing in anger.

"I rode by Moreaux's today since we hadn't seen him for a time and saw his frozen body lying out by his corral. His horses were all half-starved and I gave them grain. Jules had a ball-hole in his forehead. I went inside the house, calling for his mis-

116

sus but she didn't answer. I found her in the kitchen.
Her windpipe was crushed and . . . and . . . God, it
was horrible."

Chollie struggled to keep his emotions in check,
but his voice grew raspy and trailed off.

"What about tha' snowshoe?" asked Faron
MacGregor.

"It's Horne's," said Reinhardt, speaking for the
first time. He tossed it to MacGregor. "I found its
mate leaning in front of Horne's door. Horne is
gone."

"Gone?" gasped a half dozen men.

"And, my daughter with him, the bastard,"
shrieked Lou Simmons. "Maybe he murdered her
too!"

"Now calm down, Lou," said Chollie. "We've got
to sift through all this and not jump to conclusions."

Reinhardt watched quietly as the men argued
and fought over scraps of information like a pack
of hungry dogs. He suppressed a smile, but his
lips curved with a satisfaction he could scarcely
conceal.

"I think we do have to jump to conclusions,"
said Reinhardt, his strong voice commanding attention from the others. "We have a murdered
family here in the valley, and a man missing. All
of Horne's stock is gone. Why would a man run,
unless he were guilty?"

"Moreaux's furs were gone, too," said Chollie.
"I know he had some prime pelts in his shed. I
looked and they were plumb gone."

"I say we go after him," said Bill McPherson,
his neck swelled like a bull elk in the rut, his face
flushed with a suffusion of blood in his capillaries.
"Hunt him down and hang him."

"Go after him in the dead of winter?" asked
MacGregor.

"He's got my daughter," muttered Simmons, scratching underneath the bush of his beard.

Reinhardt stepped into the ragged circle of men. He held up his hands as if to keep the tide of angry words from washing over him.

"Listen, friends," he said, his voice sliding on smooth oil, unctuous as honey, "there's no need to go off at the half-cock. Horne is a thief and a killer, we know that. But, he will return. His place is still here. He will wait until we cool down, maybe in the spring, and he'll come back."

"He's right," said Chollie. "Horne wouldn't leave this valley for very long."

"What if he's kilt my daughter?" whined Simmons, his eyes rolled back in their sockets.

"I don't think he has," said Reinhardt. "He would have left some sign. No, I think he took her along as a hostage, so we wouldn't come after him. If we did follow him, he might kill her, though."

Reinhardt let them think about that for a moment.

"We'll be ready for him when he comes back!" shouted McPherson.

"That's the spirit," said Reinhardt. "This is our valley and there's no place in it for a man like Horne. He'll be back. And we'll be ready for him."

Simmons spluttered, but the men calmed him down.

"Lou, break out some whiskey," said Chollie. "What we all need is a drink."

This suggestion brought a cheer from the assemblage. Simmons walked behind a counter, brought up a corked jug, set it on the counter. The men crowded around him as he set out cups. Chollie pulled the cork, began to pour.

Simmons lifted his cup.

"We'll get him, by gum. We'll get Horne. At last, and this valley will grow into a decent, God-fearing town. I'll have my daughter back and she'll marry and live decent."

"Hear, hear!" shouted Faron and the others joined in with huzzahs as they downed their drinks.

"We've got to organize," said Chollie. "Make us a town like Lou said. We'll elect us a mayor, and a council, maybe, and a sheriff."

"Yes, a sheriff," said Campbell. "We need a sheriff."

"I agree," said Stewart. "Every town needs law and order."

"Law and order, aye," said Faron MacGregor, and Simmons poured the next round of drinks as he beamed with a satisfaction long denied him since Horne had taken his daughter away from him and Elizabeth.

Reinhardt stood back and viewed his handiwork. If anything could pull a settlement together, he thought, it was a common danger, a common enemy. He had done his work, done it well.

Horne was the enemy.

If he ever came back to the valley, the townsfolk would turn on him like a pack of wolves, devour him without batting an eye.

Horne slipped out of bed, picked up his boots and pistols, slung on his possibles pouch and pair of powder horns—one filled with fine priming powder, the other, larger, with a coarser grain. He tip-toed past Mary Lee, sleeping in her bedroll on the floor. He had not slept, but waited until her breathing was even. He made no sound as he padded like a prowling cougar to the kitchen. There he lighted a lamp, set it on the table. He checked the flints on his pistols, blew the pans clear. He pulled on his boots, slid the Spanish *miguelet* pistols onto his belt. They had flanged hooks attached to the sides, shot a .66 caliber ball. He would prime them later, if need be, using the smaller horn with the extra fine priming powder.

He pulled on his buffalo coat, squared his hat, blew out the lamp, walked to the back door and let himself out into the darkness. He let his eyes grow accustomed to the blackness, made out the shapes of the outbuildings. He walked to the barn, felt his way to a post where the lanterns were hung, a sulphur match at the ready.

A sound popped the silence in Horne's ears. A match flared and Dave's face floated out of the pitch. The glass chimney clanked as Sheppers touched his match to the wick. The lamp flared with a smoky glow.

"Thought you was asleep," drawled Horne.

"Brought something for you. Wanted to be sure you got off all right."

"I know the way."

Dave held out something in his hand. Horne recognized it after a moment as Dave hung the lantern on a ten penny square nail driven into the center post.

"I loaded the cylinders with powder and ball," said Dave. "You can cap 'em when you want."

Horne took the holster, drew the Colt's from its sheath. He turned it over in his hand, held it up to the light.

"Jimmy wanted you to have it if anything happened to him."

Horne did not speak but shoved the pistol back in the leather. Then he walked to Tony, hung the belt loop from the saddle horn.

"You might need the Colt's," said Sheppers.

"Might. You take care, Dave."

"I will."

Horne said no more. He checked the cinch on

Tony's saddle, grunted his approval. Dave handed him the lead rope attached to Gideon and Stepper. Horne led the animals out of the barn, hauled himself up into the saddle. He rode off into the darkness, looked up at the sky, took his bearings from the Big Dipper, headed south on the pale road, lit only by the thin sliver of moon, the distant starshine.

The wind blew down on the plain from the nearby mountains. Horne slipped into warm gloves and latched the top elkhorn button on his buffalo coat tight around his neck. He listened to the thump of the hooves on the ground, heard the distant cry of a coyote yapping. He felt Tony bristle under him and he spoke to the horse, his voice low and soothing.

Leaving Mary Lee behind gave him a good feeling. He felt as if a heavy pack had been lifted from his shoulders. He drew in a breath and the air tasted sweet, tasted of snowy pines and balsam, of flowing rivers and the heady tang of freedom, a man's most precious possession.

• CHAPTER 15 •

D AVE SHEPPERS KNEW RIGHT AWAY THAT SHE WAS
gone. He went out to the barn anyway, just
to make sure. The Indian pony was gone,
and so was Mary Lee Simmons. He looked to the
south and shook his head as he gazed across the
empty prairie. He didn't understand any of this
business between Horne and the girl, but he felt
the immense surge of the mysterious force that
drives the universe, pulls a man and a woman together despite any obstacles strewn in their paths.

"I hope you catch up to him, little lady," Dave
said aloud and Dancer looked over the fencerail
at him and whickered.

Horne crossed the South Platte at a narrow,
shallow ford, then followed the snow-dusted foothills which looked like sugarloafs under the shrouding mist. He was headed toward Cherry Creek. It
was colder now, the feeble sun pulling the chill from

the ground through the thick gray batting of clouds that stretched from horizon to horizon.

Once, he saw a lone buggy in the distance. It was moving slowly, like a beetle, toward the ford at the Platte. And in late afternoon a pair of boys on horses raced across the plain, and he heard their shouts only after they had disappeared behind a low hill. He skirted the settlements, crossing creek after creek, drifting ever south. Clouds clung to the mountain range and he never saw the sky all day. Antelope watched him pass through, standing like statues, their pronghorns dark against the snow, their cream and white hides the color of rocks on the hillsides.

He made camp before dark, well off the trail, far enough away from the creek so that he could barely hear it. The clouds dropped even lower, scudding down from the mountains in a silent drenching mist. He heard her coming long before he saw her and when she appeared, his fire was just beginning to warm him, the saddle blanket steaming on a flat stone.

"You could get shot riding up on a man like that," Horne told her.

"I'm cold and tired," she said.

She looked bedraggled, too, he thought, but there was no mistaking the determination in the set of her jaw as she swung down from her pony, walked toward him on wobbly legs. Later, when she had stripped her mount and hobbled the pony by the creek, he watched as she cleared the snow from a spot and dragged part of the fire over it. She built another fire, spread it out to warm the ground. Horne made bannock in the fry pan, dropped chunks of dried elk meat in the batter.

"There is only enough food for one," he said.

She looked at him sharply. "We'll make do," she

replied and knifed an airtight of peaches until he could smell the syrup.

She ate sparingly even though he had made more than he would eat by himself. The bannock was thick and meaty, the crust a golden brown. They shared the peaches, spearing the chunks with knives, slurping them down parched gullets.

"You knew I'd come," she said, as she scoured the skillet with snow before taking it to the creek with the tin dishes and eating utensils.

"I told Dave to keep you there."

"You can't keep the wind from blowing, Horne."

He laughed as she tramped through the snow to the creek. He moved the fire, laid his bedroll on the ground where it had been. He built up the new fire, sat on his blankets, watching it bounce light off the fog-cloud that hovered over the camp. Mary Lee returned, put the plates and forks away. She sat on her bedroll and looked across the fire at him.

"You want me to make coffee?" she asked.

"No."

She drew a comb from her saddlebag, began raking it through her hair. The teeth made a soft sound running through her tresses and the creek sounded like a cat purring somewhere far off, or else it was the wind building, sneaking down through the clouds like a whisper.

"You don't know what you're getting into, girl."

"I'm not a girl, Horne."

"Garcia's going to be watching his backtrail. I don't think he's in any hurry and he knows I'm coming."

She basked in the sound of his deep voice, turned her head this way and that as she combed her hair out until it shone in the firelight.

"You don't know this country," he said.

".Yes, I do," she replied, and he knew what she meant.

"That damned Red Hawk," Horne muttered.

Mary Lee said nothing. She put her comb away and pulled off her moccasins, crinkled her toes before the fire, her face beauteously lit by the dancing flames.

"You don't keep up, I'll leave you behind," he said, as he stuffed his boot moccasins into his blankets.

"I know," she smiled.

Horne grunted and crawled into his bedroll.

"You look like a whipped pup," he growled.

Mary Lee smiled again, then crept into her blankets and pulled them up over her head.

The coyotes began to sing as the fire crackled and burned low, the mist drowning it ever so slowly as it hugged the snowy ground and the wind died into a deep silence.

The day was monotonous, long. South to the springs rode Horne, Mary Lee less than a hundred yards behind him, a small shadow on a paint pony, the weather cold as a hardrock miner's rump, the slanted pyramids of the Rockies jutting crazily into clouds, their bristled slopes cottoned with snow a yard thick. Pike's Peak rose majestically above the other mountains and tilted behind them as he swung east, following ancient invisible buffalo tracks that had blotted out a trail and had now become a road scarred by iron shoes and wagon wheels; and it was spattered occasionally with rotting wooden crosses where men and women had died and been buried under piled stone and brush to keep the wolves and coyotes away from the flesh that ultimately would be claimed by blind worms that made no sound in the deep ocean of earth—would be eaten away by the sudden acids that flooded the body as soon as the breath stopped and the brain emptied of thought and dream.

Horne looked at a stone mound on the sloping wave of a hill, the tilted wooden cross that had lost its footing in the grasping earth, and remembered passing by that place before when the grave had been fresh and sprinkled with blue columbines and summer brown-eyed Susans plucked hastily from a blossomed prairie. He had seen the mourners still standing there when he had passed; their faces were blank and fresh-looking but the bloom was gone from their sunken eyes, and dirty tears streaked their lean faces like the shore marks left by rivers shifting their levels. The people told Horne that one of their own, a woman from Kansas who had two small boys, had been taken by the croup after being caught in a thunderstorm out on the desolate wasteland east of Spanish Peaks. The rain had beat needles into the land and the wind tore canvas from their land schooners and lashed them with fierce whips for a day and a half, whirling little cyclones around them until they thought Ezekiel must be returning in the whirlwind to chastise them for their sins.

Horne looked at Mary Lee, knew she must be thinking of her sisters, whose ashes probably had been blown all up and down the South Platte by the winds. There were no crosses to mark their graves.

"There's folks a-comin'," said Mary Lee, shouting to be heard above the keen of the wind.

"Saw 'em."

"Don't look right, Horne."

"You got good eyes, woman."

She smirked. Horne was coming around. At least he had called her woman instead of girl. Now if he would ever use her name, she'd put more rows of Crow beads on the thing she was making for him. She had brought the rosette and the loom, thread, the precious beads she had saved from her time with the Arapaho.

The wagon grew larger in their sight as they rode. Horne saw the outriders, their rifles pointing to the sky. The people in the wagon had rifles, too, he noticed.

"You going to talk to them, Horne?" Mary Lee asked when they drew near.

"Looks like they want to talk to us." One of the outriders headed their way, his rifle outlined against the stark gray sky.

Horne reined up, waited for the approaching rider. Mary Lee rode up alongside him. He was on Stepper, Tony and Gideon were lined up single-file on the lead rope. The horses whickered, shifted their feet nervously. The snow was blown off the road and the ground was hard. Hoofbeats sounded loud under the high whine of the wind.

"Mister, you'd better turn back," said the rider as he brought his horse to a halt. "There ain't nothin' but trouble south of here."

"Who are you?" asked Horne.

"Name's Joe Doyle and I've got my family with me. We just come from Huerfano village. Everybody at the Pueblo is dead or captured. Utes are thick as fleas in the hills."

"I heard something about it."

"There ain't nobody at the mouth of the Fountain no more, just some Mexes and they ain't no better'n the Utes."

"I'd like to hear about the Mexicans," said Horne.

"Bandits."

"They bring fresh horses down in the last month?"

"They did, right after the last trouble." Doyle was anxious to talk. He kept licking dry lips under his wiry beard. Only part of his face showed under the hat. His ears were hidden by the woolen scarf bandaging his head and neck. His eyes were a pale blue. "I tell you it's been pure hell. You're Horne, ain't you?"

"I'm Horne."

"I seen you in Santa Fe once't, and I heard Baca talkin' about you a time or two."

"I know Baca."

"Him and his family moved to the St. Charles village after the Pueblo murders. Some of the traders was goin' to move farther down the Arkansas. They had their wagons loaded and ready to roll with nine Cherokee teamsters. They come through our village at Huerfano and the Utes kilt ever' one of 'em and burnt the wagons. The Injuns come on back to our village. My wife and kids was stayin' with Dick Wootten. I was off tradin' with the Arapahoes when it happened." Doyle pointed back to the wagon as it rattled up and halted. "That's my family," he said, "and a couple of friends."

The two other outriders were no more than boys, and they looked all around them, their fingers inside the trigger guards of their rifles.

"Go on," said Horne.

"When them Injuns galloped on back to the village, a gravedigger was just finishing up a hole for Rumaldo Cordova. He jumped into the grave and the Utes rode on by without seein' him. Wootten he was ready for the Injuns. He had piled sacks of corn around the edge of his roof and put men up there behind 'em with rifles cocked. He had a bunch of men on horseback behind the gate of his *placita*. When the Injuns come, they gave 'em hell. A dozen men rode out shootin' and the men on the roof opened fire. Them Injuns pulled out of there like a pack of scalded cats."

"I'm glad your family wasn't hurt," said Horne.

"We lost three men. But they was against nigh two hunnert Ute and Jicarilly, Blanco and that Apache chief, Guero."

"Those horses you saw with the Mexicans. They still got 'em?"

"Far as I know. Garcia's got him a stronghold somewhere up the Fountain."

"Those are my horses," Horne told him.

Doyle whistled.

"He's got him a dozen men at least. One of 'em a Frenchie used to come by the villages. Jacques something."

"Berthoud," said Horne.

"Yeah. And Delgado, he's one of 'em."

"I'll be on my way, then," said Horne.

"It ain't safe," said Doyle. "Nowhere down there is safe no more."

Horne touched a finger to the brim of his hat and rode past Doyle and the outriders. He nodded to the woman and her children in the wagon. Mary Lee dropped behind Gideon, bringing up the rear. They were stopped by a shout from Doyle.

"Horne!"

Horne hauled in on the reins, turned his horse. He looked back at Doyle.

"Yeah?"

"Garcia's got men all along this trail. I seen two of 'em this mornin'. They let us pass, but I don't think you'll be so lucky."

"I'll keep that in mind," said Horne. "Thanks."

"So long, Horne. Miss."

"*Adios,*" said Horne.

"They'll be about five miles down the road," yelled Doyle as Horne pulled away.

As it turned out, Garcia's men were only three miles away, and when Horne saw them he noticed they were both riding horses that belonged to him.

·CHAPTER 16·

HORNE RECOGNIZED THE HORSES. ONE WAS A SOR-
rel gelding he called Comanche, the other,
a black mare he had named Rosie. The two
Mexicans looked out of place on their backs. The
men held short-barreled plains rifles across their
pommels. Their saddlehorns dripped with pistols.
Slickers and bedrolls were lashed behind the cantles of their Santa Fe vaquero saddles, Spanish-
rigged with *tapaderos* and single horse-hair
cinches. Rosie, Horne remembered, had some
trouble with her hoof a while back, she had
slashed the frog on her right forehoof when she
had stepped on a buffalo skull and shattered it.
She favored it now, although the middle cleft of
the frog had long since healed.

"Mary Lee," said Horne, "you ride up along on
my left side."

"What're you going to do?" she asked.

"Talk to 'em if I can."

"Horne, be careful."

"Just ride close," he said.

The Mexicans waited for them. They halted their horses on the hillside, sat their saddles with an assured arrogance. The wind fluttered their wide hatbrims, blew at their coats so that the matted buffalo hair ruffled like feathers.

Horne looked into the dark hollows of their eye-sockets, took in their stern attitudes, the way their gloved hands held their rifles, fingers curled around triggers. But no rifle had been cocked yet, no threat had been made.

The Mexicans rode down the hill, took command of the road, bracing it so that Horne could not pass.

"Do you have tobacco, *Señor?*" asked one of the Mexicans of Horne, his accent thick, the tonal quality of his voice a liquid whine.

"No," said Horne, reining in his horse. Mary Lee stopped a horse-stride behind him.

"Ah, then maybe you have a taste of whiskey for us? It makes much cold."

"I don't have any whiskey, either," said Horne. "Those are fine horses you ride."

"He likes our horses, Miguel," said the second Mexican, grinning with long yellowed teeth. "We have many more like these," he said to Horne.

"He has fine horses, too, Pablito," said the first Mexican. "Maybe you want to buy some or sell one of yours," he told Horne.

"I have plenty of horses," said Horne. "Those are mine you are riding."

The expressions on the Mexicans' faces changed suddenly. They brought up their rifles quickly, cocking them. Horne drew the Colt's .44 that had belonged to Jimmy Hemphill. Mary Lee shrieked a warning.

"It is Horne!" yelled Pablito.

"Kill him!" from Miguel.

The Mexicans pulled the triggers. The hammers

fell on ignition caps. Flame and smoke belched from their plains rifles. Horne fired the pistol, felt it buck in his hand as the first cap exploded the powder. He fired again even as he felt a hammering pain in his leg. His horse shuddered under him and went down like a pole-axed steer, pitching him into the cloud of white smoke. He hit the ground hard. His left shoulder took the shock and shoots of pain coursed through the collarbone.

He saw the shadowy figures of the Mexicans through the smoke and brought the pistol up, cocking as he tried to aim. He fired again, saw Miguel lurch in the saddle, heard him cry out.

"*Vámonos!*" yelled Pablito.

Horne heard the horses wheel and gallop away, their hoofs thudding on the packed earth of the road. He fired another shot in the general direction of the riders, but the pain in his shoulder made him wince with the buck of the pistol.

"You shot one of them," shouted Mary Lee.

Horne grunted and keeled over, giddy from loss of blood. He felt the shearing pain in his shinbone, the hot slide of wet blood down his leg.

Mary Lee jumped from her pony, rushed to Horne, pulled him away from the quivering horse.

"You're hurt," she said.

"Shoot Stepper," he groaned. "Take my pistol and put the muzzle in his ear."

"Horne. . . ."

He pushed her away, crawled over to the horse. Its muzzle was shot half away, slivers of bone jutted through the mangled meat. Horne put the pistol up to its ear and pulled the trigger. The animal kicked with one last reflex and then was still. Horne closed his eyes, sucked in a deep breath. He wrestled with his possibles pouch, brought it around to his lap. He started to pull out the powder horn to reload his pistol when a wave of nausea washed over him. Bile stung his throat.

"Mary Lee," he gasped.

She knelt by him, looked at his blood-drenched leg. The right shin glistened with ropes of crimson, bright bubbles oozing from a single hole.

"I've got to get you to a doctor," she said.

Horne, groggy with pain, woozy from loss of blood, shook his head.

"We've got to get the hell out of here," he said. "Those were Garcia's men, for sure. They'll be back to finish with me."

"Where can we go? You're bleeding bad."

"To the springs. A creek. Someplace where there's water and I can hole up."

"Yes, I know a place," she said, looking off to the mountains.

"Take the saddle off Stepper, put it on Tony. Can you do that?"

"Yes."

"Then you better ride on back."

"Back? No. I can't leave you, Horne. I won't leave you."

Too weak to protest, Horne slumped over, unable to reload the Colt's. He fought off the nausea, the deathly crawl of shadows in his brain as Mary Lee went in and out of focus, as everything blurred together like chips of glass in a kaleidoscope all tumbling at once.

He tried to speak, but he heard no sound from his lips and he wondered if he was dreaming because the shadows had come now and shut out all the light of his thoughts as if someone had snuffed a lamp in a solitary room, plunging it into darkness. He heard far-off sounds, but he could make no sense of them. They were jumbled up and might have been bats flying from a cave at dusk, or leather door hinges squealing and creaking or just summer grasses being riffled by the wind. . . .

Mary Lee knew she had to stop the bleeding before she did anything else. Horne lay sprawled on the frozen ground, his face strangely pale, his leg gushing blood. Yet, there was danger here if the Mexicans came back. Quickly, she tore a strip from the rebozo she wore around her hips. She tied a tourniquet above the shin wound, found an oblong slender stone to use as a tightening lever. She twisted the stone until the blood stopped flowing, pulled Horne away from the dead horse and lay him out flat, his feet higher than his head. She felt the wound, found that the ball had gone clean through his leg. The flesh was blown away at the back and the sight made her woozy. She wrapped the shredded rebozo around the wound. For now, it would have to do.

She loosened the cinch on Stepper's saddle, dragged it out from under the dead hulk. She stripped the bridle off, the leather slippery with blood. She saddled Tony as the seconds ticked away with maddening speed. The horse was skittery, but she tightened the cinch, led the animal over close to Horne.

She rubbed snow on Horne's face and brought him back to consciousness.

"You've got to get on Tony," she said breathlessly. "Hurry."

Horne struggled to clear his head, to regain his senses. She helped him to his feet. There was no pain now, just a sharp throbbing in his leg where the tourniquet dug into his flesh. He swore and grabbed the saddle horn, tugged himself into the seat. He swore again as he swung his wounded leg over the cantle.

"Let's go," he grunted.

Mary Lee grabbed the lead rope, pulled Gideon up close as she mounted the pinto. Horne held onto the saddlehorn with both hands, slumped over the saddle. Mary Lee grabbed his reins, pulled Tony along with her and Gideon. She rode into the foothills, heading west, then veering north away from Pueblo.

Horne said nothing as they rode into the snowy timber and circled. Every so often, Mary Lee stopped and loosened the tourniquet, then tightened it again. At least, she thought, the blood was clotting. The cold helped and she was later able to remove the tourniquet and wrap the strand of cloth around the wound so that she could watch it for signs of fresh bleeding.

She saw the tracks on the snowswept game trail, knew what they were without thinking about it. Red Hawk had shown her so much when they were together. She knew this trail and she knew the pony tracks that had ground up the snow belonged to a very large party of Indians, probably Utes at this time of year since the Arapaho would be far out on the plains, at one of the forts, or along the Arkansas. The tracks sent a cold chill up her spine.

She sought higher ground, forsook the game trail and kept to the windblown rimrock paths that would leave few tracks. She used all the tricks she had learned from the Arapaho, hiding her trail, stopping often to listen and moving slowly through the timber, looping back to check her backtrail. Satisfied, she headed her pony still higher to a place of bubbling springs, a meandering creek that grew from the trickle of water oozing from the stone.

Mary Lee helped Horne dismount, lay out his bedroll, led the groggy man there, put him down. She covered him with blankets, checked his bandages. There was no fresh bleeding and she breathed a deep, relieved sigh before leaving him.

She cut spruce boughs for a temporary shelter, made a small camp after hobbling the horses, tying Gideon to a deadfall pine on a long rope. She grained the animals, made sure they could get to water downstream. She made a fire under the shelter so the smoke would break up as it rose through the needles.

When the shelter was warm, she dragged Horne, still atop his bedroll, inside and unwrapped the strips of her rebozo. She cleaned his wounds, packed them with creek mud and clay from the mouth of the spring thawed at the fire. This was a good place to be, she thought, amid the towering pines, closed in by the clumps of spruce and occasional fir, like a woodland chapel, silent, majestic, a place of ancient Indian spirits hushed under a mantle of purest snow.

"Lie still," she told him, "so the wounds will scab over and start to heal."

"The Arapaho learned you well," he said, his voice weak, barely audible.

"Yes."

"I lived with 'em, too."

"I know."

"Good people once."

"Shh. Be still."

He looked at her, woozy from loss of blood, and she did not break the glance. Their gazes locked in mortal combat for a long moment. In the swirling depths of their eyes, there were questions, challenges.

Horne closed his eyes. His leg felt cool, the pain dulled by the soothing mud pack, the healing clay. Mary Lee fed the fire and brought the saddlebags and packs inside the shelter. She made a brothy stew and kept it hot for Horne. She shivered, not from cold, but from fear. She did not know if Horne would heal so fast this time. Later, she ate some of the stew, crawled inside his blankets and felt warm.

* * *

On the third day in the shelter, the gray clouds turned black as they massed over the mountains. The temperature dropped and the winds began to stir, gusting and whining off the rimrock above them, whipping the fire, shaking the spruce limbs.

"Horne," she said, touching his fevered forehead tenderly, "there is a storm brewing. I know of a cabin nearby. I must take you there."

He groaned, looked at her with glazed, red-rimmed eyes cloudy with a distant pain.

"How do you know about this cabin?"

"Red Hawk rode through here. He knew where all the settlers lived and where their dwellings were."

"Who lives in this cabin?" he rasped.

"Nobody—anymore," she said. She lowered her head, avoiding his gaze.

Horne sucked in a breath. He looked through the boughs at the sky, knew she was right about the storm. By tomorrow the snow would be flying. He was weak and hurting bad again. The ball had grazed bone, but his leg was intact. That was in his favor. Mary Lee had cleaned the wound with cold water, repacked it with spring clay and mud, but it would have to be bandaged if they were going to move.

"Yes," he said. "We'll go."

She lifted her head, looked into his eyes. Her lips quivered into a faint smile.

"I'll get the horses saddled," she said.

"Just one," he told her. "Tony. He'll pack double if it's not too far."

"It's not far, Horne."

Horne nodded in surrender to the will of this woman who would not leave him be and who now held an unwelcome power over him.

• CHAPTER 17 •

THE CABIN WASN'T MUCH; A HASTILY BUILT SHELter thrown together by some prospector, later occupied by a family whose bones were probably scattered all over the mountainside. Horne didn't want to think about the fact that Mary Lee probably had been there before with Red Hawk. The cabin was high up on a slope, next to a skinny creek. But there was a lean-to for the animals, and a built-in bunk that was still intact, slatted with thick pine that had cured hard. The others had rotted away, their boards lying scattered on the uneven dirt and rock floor. There was a fireplace and chimney, infested with squealing rats protesting the intrusion. The room smelled of animal offal and the musty aroma of decay.

Mary Lee laid out their bedrolls, made the bunk up for Horne. He lay on it in exhaustion, closed his eyes. In seconds he was asleep, the throb of his leg like a pulse at his temple. It had taken them half a day to ride five miles through the snow over fallen timber, following the narrow, treacherous trail.

She gathered wood, broke up the rotted boards for kindling, started a fire. Smoke billowed down the chimney, and she had to clean out the debris before it would draw. Chinks in the walls let the cold air in, but gradually, the air began to warm.

The storm hit the next day. Snow blew down full force off the mountain, drifted high, locked them in tight. The cold turned deadly and Horne shivered in his sleep. Mary Lee stoked the fire, moved her blankets to the bunk. She crawled in with Horne. Her body heat kept him warm.

Horne sank into delirium, dreamed the bad dreams. He fought the old battles with Red Hawk and Garcia. And, there were the shadows of women in his dreams, Sleeping Water and the woman in Santa Fe, Perla Luz.

Mary Lee heard him call out their names and winced under the onslaught of a terrible dread. Horne's fever raged and she had to bring more wood inside the cabin, tend to the animals in wind that blew out her senses, drove her back to the fire every few moments to burn off the murderous chill that knifed to her core.

The storm lasted almost a week. Mary Lee nursed Horne back to health, nurtured him with hot broth and scalding coffee, broke his fever with cold snow rubbed into his naked flesh, poured boiled water into him when it was cool enough to drink so that he would not dehydrate.

Maybe the stillness awoke him. Although it was still snowing, the howling wind had died away. The cabin shivered in the quiet, frosty patches in every corner, icicles over the cracks in the walls.

Mary Lee was asleep next to him. They were

both naked. She was soft and warm, her skin like silk next to his. He felt her electricity crackling on his flesh and his heart pumped hard with a throbbing beat. The pain in his leg had gone away and there was only a tenderness there as long as he kept it still. He was hungry, but there was another yearning in him now—one that had been buried, forgotten. The scent of her hair stirred the memories of the other women and the earthy aroma of her bare skin dank with nightsweat made him giddy with the closeness of her.

She opened her eyes slowly and turned to look at him, face to face.

Horne smiled wanly. Her breath washed across his face as she let out a deep sigh. She moved against him and he could not hide the way he felt.

"Horne?"

"Yes, dammit," he answered huskily.

"You mean it?"

"You know damned well I do."

"Don't—don't hurt me," she said softly.

"No."

"Oh God, Horne, if you only knew how I've wanted this moment."

She put her arms around him, kissed him on the mouth. Something went out of him, then. But also, something came into him: an excitement, a thrill, a challenge, a fear. Her kiss wiped out the past and blossomed a future he had not imagined. Something powerful and vital surged within him. Swift hands seemed to take his soft clay, the lost, forgotten clay of him, and shape it, knead it anew, pluck it, stroke it, spread it wide and give it spine and substance.

She breathed life into him.

They were no longer strangers, naked and ashamed. Horne no longer looked through Mary

Lee, but at her—his gaze lingering on her features
like moss or mistletoe, clinging to special places:
her mouth, her hair, her tummy, her slender legs,
the mystery between them. Maybe it was the
closeness of the snow-vaulted cabin, the intimacy
of peril, but he was drawn to her, fascinated by
her, drunk on her sudden beauty. It was as if she
had emerged from the woody cocoon and become
a butterfly. It wasn't that he had never noticed her
before. It was just that he now noticed that she
was a woman and that she was beautiful.

"Sometimes," he told her, "you smell like ripe
apples in the fall. You know, when apples are in
the cellar in barrels, fresh-picked and sweet, tast-
ing like wine."

She glowed with his talk and delicately drew
the comb through her tresses on their sixth night
of confinement in the abandoned cabin. The firelight daubed her face with copper and gold, made
her hair shine russet.

He leaned down and sniffed her hair, burrowed
his nose in deep at the nape of her neck.

"And, sometimes, when you wash your hair, you
smell like honey."

She shivered. "I haven't washed my hair."

"It smells washed."

"That's you," she laughed and he crumpled her
hair in his hands and kissed her behind the ear
until she shivered and rose up from the bench, put
her arms around his waist, drew him against her.

"You are a sinful woman."

"Not any more sinful than you, Horne."

"You're a temptress in pigtails."

"I'm not a baby. I'm a woman, good as any," she
said firmly.

"Yes, God yes," he growled low in his throat.

Her laughter echoed in the cabin, ancient as sin,

merry as the pipes of Pan, seductive as a siren's song.

Over the following days of healing, as Horne dug a path from the cabin to the lean-to, brought in firewood, carried water from the creek to the stock and for their own use, he fell more deeply in love with her, became even more bewildered by her.

"You could grow on a man," he told her one day, when he was massaging his leg wound. The bullet had missed the shin, torn only flesh. Again, he had been lucky.

"I want to grow on you," she replied. She had put away her beadwork moments before, when Horne returned from the creek carrying two snowshoe rabbits from his snares. They were gutted out and skinned, hanging inside to cure for a day.

"Mary Lee, you're still just a kid."

"I'm a woman grown, Horne. I've told you that before. Showed you, too, I reckon."

He pulled his legging back on, laced up his boot moccasin. Some days he felt old. This was one of those days. Mary Lee seemed to be growing younger by the minute. With her fresh-scrubbed face, her radiant hair, the sprinkling of freckles around her nose, she looked almost child-like in the dim light of the room. Last night she had told him she wanted to be his woman forever. Now that he was gnawing at his own foot in the trap, he had begun to wonder at his good fortune. Things could change mighty fast when a man fell for a woman. Everything got twisted out of proportion, like a bear track in the woods. If a man had a good rifle and plenty of powder and ball, the track seemed mighty small. If he had only a knife and not a climbing tree within a hundred yards, the track might grow into a twelve-foot silvertip she-grizzly's. With cubs.

"Why would you want to give up your family, the decent upbringing they gave you, to throw in with me?" he asked. "What did Red Hawk do to you?"

"Red Hawk beat me, Horne. Every day. Every night. He treated me like one of the camp dogs. Is that what you wanted to know?"

"No." He sensed that the edge to her voice masked an anger that bordered on hysteria. He wanted no part of such outbursts. They had already been in the damned cabin too long, but the snows were deep and he had heard an avalanche in the night, a deadly muffled roar that could not have been more than a mile from them.

"I shouldn't have asked. It doesn't matter."

"Yes, Horne, yes it does," she said quickly.

"Maybe I don't want to hear about it then," he said.

She scrunched her mouth into a fist-like glower and her eyes narrowed to a pair of fierce slits.

"I was the youngest among my sisters," she said. "Pa and Ma raised us strict. But, there wasn't much love there. Not the kind I could feel and touch and hold close in my breast. When Red Hawk took us away, he paid me more mind than my folks. Horne, I hated him. But, I—I felt something inside me, too. Something strange, a quivering like, a scared kind of yearning.

"He hurt me, but he took me to his bed and there was just the two of us and I imagined that he loved me in a kind of odd way and that made me feel good. I cried myself to sleep at night, but when he touched me in his sleep, I trembled all over with my desire for him."

"Christ," said Horne. "I don't want to know all this."

"No, Horne, I'm going to finish. Please. I've thought of little else since you brought me back. Red Hawk, for all his badness, had a magic, a power, over me. When he walked through the camp, the people looked at him like he was a god. I could feel it, see it. I felt the same way about him whenever I saw him strut and swagger, throw out his chest and lift his arrogant savage head high. He was like lightning that hits you again and again. He had something inside him that was magnetic. He—he did things to me that made me forget all the hurt, the pain."

Horne thought he knew what she was talking about. He had seen men kick dogs, beat them brutally, and the dogs responded with love and affection. Worship, even. It was a strange thing to witness, like seeing a sow devour one of her brood while nursing a half dozen others. Mary Lee's admission jolted him, nonetheless.

"Well, Horne," she said, "you are much like Red Hawk. Only I see a goodness in you that was not in him. A gentleness, too. You have that magic inside you, though. That magnet. Drawing people to you. Making them respect you."

Horne snorted. "Mary Lee, I think you got hit in the head just one too many times."

"No, I'm not crazy, Horne. I know what I see. And what I feel. I had wounds when you brought me back. Bad as the ones you've had. Worse, maybe. I had to let them heal. They were deep. I couldn't cry out. I couldn't scream. I wanted to, but I couldn't, I was hurt too bad. You let me heal. You kept quiet so I could keep quiet—and I didn't have to scream and tear out my hair by the roots. You think your leg hurts? Nothing hurts like the soul that's been crushed underfoot."

Horne heaved a deep and heavy sigh. As much as he cared for her, he also was struck by the re-

144

alization that there was no escaping her. The more he kicked her, the stronger the bond between them would be. She wouldn't go away. And she wouldn't listen to reason. Mary Lee was attached to him, and maybe he to her. If he wanted to be rid of her, he had to figure out how to make her go away without being cruel. But did he really want that? He buried the question in the loam of his mind, stamped it down deep with the heel of his conscious thought.

"What's going to happen to us, Horne?" she asked.

"I don't know," he said. "But if the weather don't break, we'll be here 'til spring. And maybe we won't get out then."

She knew what he meant. Their food supplies were dwindling. Horne could not get out to hunt. The horses were low on grain.

"I mean, when we get out."

"I've got things to do," he said.

"Horne, you are a caution. You are bullheaded."

"Maybe."

"No, you remind me of a sign I saw in St. Louis once. It was in a store window. Pa and I were rushing by when I stopped and showed it to him. He didn't even laugh. He said he didn't understand it. In some ways you're just like him."

"What did the sign say?" asked Horne.

"It said 'Slow down, Sir. The thing you're rushing to may not be as important as the thing you're passing by.' "

"I understand it," he told her, "but seems to me it fits some of your doin's same as mine."

"Jackson Horne, you're not only bullheaded, you're pigheaded. I know what I'm going after and I know what I'm passing by."

He swallowed it, all of it. He may have suppressed the question, but he looked toward Mary Lee more kindly and began to treat her better. He didn't want a whipped dog following him about. If she was going to take up with him, he wanted it to be for a better reason than Red Hawk had given her.

• CHAPTER 18 •

THE THAW CAME A WEEK LATER, AND EVEN IF IT hadn't, Horne knew he and Mary Lee had to get out. The horses were down to their last hatfuls of grain, the snares hadn't been tripped in two days. They had eaten the last of the dried vegetables and the elk jerky wouldn't last more than three or four more days.

"I'll saddle up," he told Mary Lee. "You get the gear packed and meet me outside the cabin."

"How long will you be?" she asked.

"Half hour."

"I'll be ready."

Horne looked at her oddly, but she turned away from him. He shrugged and stepped outside into the bitter cold.

Mary Lee brought out her beadwork, sat down in a chair. She put the finishing touches on the bracelet she had made from old rose and greasy blue real beads with brain-tanned spacers. It very nearly matched the bracelet she wore, but was wider, stronger. She wove the leather thongs into the warp strands, strung mandril beads and knotted the leather so they would not fall off. She held the finished bracelet up to the light, turned it slowly in her hand. The bright colors dazzled her and she smiled with satisfaction. She put the bracelet aside and began to pack the parfleches, the saddlebags. She carried them outside, stacked them near the door. It was cold, but she had donned two shirts, wore a fur coat, buffalo gloves, elkhide leggings, no socks.

She went back into the cabin and retrieved the bracelet, her heart thrumming in her chest, the blood pulsing at her temples. Her hands shook as she clasped the bracelet to her bosom.

"Stop your trembling," she told herself.

She waited for Horne's call and when it came, she jumped. Uncertainty gripped her as she opened the door. He stood outside with her pinto saddled, Gideon's panniers loaded with the few goods they had left, cooking utensils, food, clothing, blankets. Tony stood hipshot, the lead rope coiled around the saddlehorn.

"Mount up," said Horne.

"Ju-just a minute," she said. "I—I've got something I want to give you."

Horne hiked her saddlebags back of her saddle, turned to look at her. Mary Lee had her hands behind her back. She stood in front of the door, shifting her weight on her feet awkwardly.

"What's that?"

"Come here," she said.

"Mary Lee, we've got a long ride down to the flat."

"Please, Horne. Don't say anything, just come here a minute."

Horne stalked over to her, a scowl visible on his

face despite the scarf that covered his ears and chin.

"Hold out your left arm," she said. "Give me your wrist."

"We don't have time for any tomfoolery, Mary Lee."

"Horne."

Reluctantly, he held out his left hand, rolled the sleeve of his sheepskin jacket up a few inches.

"This is something I made for you," she said, holding out the beaded bracelet. She tied it to his wrist, then showed him the one she wore on her own arm.

"Where did you get that?" he asked.

"I made it," she said.

"No, I mean the one on your arm."

"It was given to me by Red Hawk."

"You were his woman, then." There, he'd said it. He'd been afraid to say the words all this time.

"Yes," she sighed. "I was his woman."

"And now you want to be my woman."

"Yes."

"What did he call you?" he asked.

"Sun Hair."

"Good name." He wanted to swear, to curse Red Hawk and his damned bracelet. He knew what it was. An Arapaho love bracelet. He knew the design, had seen it before on another woman's wrist. Sleeping Water had worn one just like it and he had made her give it back to Red Hawk. He thought of Sleeping Water now, how she had died, how Red Hawk had given her to the Mexicans for more whiskey. The thought made his blood percolate dangerously. "That makes you his woman, you know."

"I don't wear it for him," she said.

"No matter. You ain't Sun Hair no more."

"He called you Gray Wolf. I know that. He said

you were a very brave man. He said that once you lived in the mountains and that you were very feared among your own kind."

"He told you these things?"

"Yes. He spoke of you to others of the tribe. And they honored him because they knew you were hunting him and it was good to be hunted by a brave man. By Gray Wolf."

"You've got to give up these things," he said. "You've got to forget the past."

"Can you? Do you?"

"I try to," said Horne.

"So do I."

He looked at the beaded bracelet on his wrist, tried to quell the bitterness that rose up in him. Mary Lee was right. He was no better than she. He could not forget Red Hawk and neither could she. Red Hawk had been a part of their lives in different ways, was a part of their lives even now. He was dead, but some parts of him lived on in their hearts. Killing him had not blurred his moccasin tracks. Red Hawk stood between them. He was in the beads and the warp, the leather and the symbols on these bracelets. Horne wanted to tear the accursed thing from his wrist and scatter its torn parts to the four directions and the winds. He wanted to blot out every trace of Red Hawk, grind him into dust and oblivion for eternity.

"I do not want you to talk about Red Hawk to me anymore," he said. "I do not want to hear his name ever again."

"Horne," she said, "I have known only two men. Red Hawk and Gray Wolf."

"Goddamnit! I'm not Gray Wolf anymore. I never was!"

"Yes," she said, "you were, and you still are. In the hearts of the Arapaho."

"You just can't give it up, can you, Mary Lee?"

150

"No. Any more than I can give up my blood, my heart, the things in my mind. And neither can you."

"We can't live that way anymore," said Horne. "The white man can't live the way the Indians do."

"I don't want to," she said. "I just want to live with you. Whatever way. Wherever."

"Mary Lee, we're just not suited to each other."

"In the blankets we are suited to each other."

"Yes, there."

"Why just there? Why not everywhere? Anywhere?"

"Because," he said. But he could not answer her.

"Will you wear my bracelet?" she asked.

"I'll wear it. Because you made it. For me. But I don't like the one you wear."

"Because Red Hawk gave it to me?"

"Not only that," he said.

"What, then?"

"It's a reminder to me of what happened to you. What happened to your sisters. Can't you see that?"

"It doesn't remind me of them. It doesn't remind me of the bad times. It reminds me of what was in Red Hawk's heart, the good part."

He had no answer for her. He had no answer at all.

He pulled his sleeve down and turned on his heel.

"Come on," he said, a tempered gruffness in his voice. "We'll talk no more of these things."

"Yes," she breathed. "Yes, we will."

Horne did not hear her. He heard only the sea-wash of his own anger in his temples as the blood rushed hard through his veins, drummed in his ears like a roaring tide, smothering all outside sounds.

* * *

Chollie Winder whacked the table in Mc-
Gonigle's with the bung-starter, pounding the
wood noisily in his entreaty for silence. Men clus-
tered in small groups, talking like steam-driven
buzz-saws, smoking, drinking from tankards and
cups, gesticulating with shaggy, coat-festooned
arms like a scattered phalanx of scarecrows in a
windstorm. The room smelled of sawdust soggy
from snowmelt, percolating sour mash, stewed
hops, alcohol, cigar and pipe smoke, dried beans
and smouldering bin-stored onions—all threaded
together with the oleaginous stench of burning
coal oil from the lamps that gorged on the sparse
oxygen in the air-tight haze around the iron stove.
"Hear, hear," he bellowed. "It's settled then.
Dan Reinhardt is the sheriff of Sky Valley. Lou
Simmons is mayor. Now, we have other business,
gentlemen."
"We have the law now," shouted Bill McPherson. "And I say the first order of business is to
bring Jackson Horne to justice."
"Seems to me that's the new mayor's job," said
Chollie. "Lou?"
Louis Simmons cleared his throat, jiggling the
wattled skin on his Adam's apple. He stepped up
to the table. Faron MacGregor puffed on his pipe,
watching the proceedings. He sat aloof from the
other men who ringed the potbellied stove in
McGonigle's. He was the only one who had voted
nay when the matter of electing a sheriff came up.
He didn't like Dan Reinhardt much and he didn't
like the idea of finding a man guilty before he was
given his day in court. But the people of Sky Valley were bound and determined to have their own
government and he had gone along with that part
of it. He would have rather seen Chollie elected
sheriff than Reinhardt.
"I'm proud to be your mayor," said Simmons.

"You all know how I feel about this valley. It's got to be made decent for folks. That's why I'm glad we got us a sheriff. I think Dan Reinhardt is just the man to carry out the law hereabouts."

"Hear, hear!" yelled McPherson, ruddy-faced from liquor. Other men chorused him until Simmons banged the bung-starter once again for silence.

"I say we rid the valley of Horne," said Simmons, "and now's a good time as any. He's kilt two of our dearest citizens and it would do my heart good to see him hang from a juniper. Not only that, he's done kidnapped little Mary Lee, my onliest daughter what's left to me."

"Run him out!" shouted a man named Fred Barris, who had come there in the fall with his wife and two sons. He was just one of many recent newcomers to Sky Valley who had been lured here by the talk of a town, school, a church, economic prosperity. Barris was a former church deacon and had promised to give bible studies to the few children, write to ministers offering them a ready-to-pray-to-Jesus flock in the wilderness.

"How do you expect to get Horne if he's already left?" asked McPherson.

"He'll come back," said Simmons. "But we don't want him back. It's high time we got some more decent settlers in here. Not only is Horne a murderer, he has been living in sin. He has sullied my daughter, shorn her of her virtue."

"Ah, Lou, you dinna know that for sure," said Faron. " 'Tis your daughter's own choice to take up with the mon."

"Not so!" exclaimed Simmons. "He's kept her against her will."

"What say you, Sheriff Reinhardt?" asked McPherson.

153

Simmons blinked, then nodded to the younger man.

"There's several ways you can get rid of Horne," he said. "You can kill him if he ever comes back and it wouldn't be against the law. You can hunt him down and kill him. Or you can try him for murder and kill him. But the only way to rid the valley of him is to kill him because you can't make him go away and stay away."

"Kill him without a fair trial?" asked Faron.

"Did he give Jules Moreaux or his wife a fair trial?" asked Reinhardt.

"We could do it another way," said Chollie. "We could bring in some more hunters and trappers. Let them work all Horne's territory, take out the game."

"That would hurt us too, mon," said Mac-Gregor.

"Temporarily, maybe," said Chollie. "Look, you want a man to move, you spoil his life for him."

"He'd buck you," said Reinhardt, breaking in quickly. "Horne won't lay hisself down for such. I say we hang him, or shoot him to death. I don't care how, but he's got to have his lights put out."

"What'll become of Horne's spread?" asked MacGregor.

"I'll take it," answered Reinhardt.

"The spoils of war," said Kurt Jaeger, speaking for the first time. His chiseled, smooth-shaven face was marred by the sneer on his lips. Everyone there knew that Dan Reinhardt was Kurt's brother-in-law. Jaeger and Reinhardt's sister moved to Sky Valley right after the trouble, after Horne had tracked down Red Hawk. Reinhardt had accompanied his sister and brother-in-law.

MacGregor looked at Reinhardt and Jaeger and wondered if the settlers had not brought in wolves to tend their sheep.

"You'll not take down Horne so easily," said MacGregor. "And unless you give the mon a fair trial, you're no better than he—murderers the lot of you."

"You keep out of this, Faron MacGregor," said McPherson. "I think we should have gotten rid of Horne a long time ago. When he came back with Mary Lee and shot Luke Newcastle. That was murder to my eyes and we let the bastard get away with it."

"What I hear," said Jaeger, "is that Horne's not really a part of this valley. Just a squatter."

"And, by all the heathen gods, what air we?" asked MacGregor. "The same, aye." He puffed his pipe angrily, spewing clouds of smoke into the air around his face.

Every man-jack in the room began to argue until Lou Simmons hammered on the tabletop with the bung-starter.

"I've made my decision," the mayor croaked hoarsely as the din died away. "Dan Reinhardt, as duly elected sheriff of Sky Valley, you are ordered to do everything in your power to drive Horne out or bring him to trial or kill him if he tries to shoot his way out."

Many of the men in the room cheered.

"I'll do that," said Reinhardt smugly. "Leave Horne to me. If I need to deputize any of you, I hope you'll back me up."

MacGregor muttered a low curse.

Simmons's eyes glittered like sunstruck agates when he declared the meeting over. Reinhardt and Jaeger huddled together in one corner of the room. The others began to fill their cups with whiskey.

Faron MacGregor left the meeting place without a word. He went home to his wife, Heather, and told her what had happened.

"It'll be foul play if those two Germans take the

law into their own hands. And it's all done for greed, not for justice."

"You jist stay out of it, Faron MacGregor," said his wife, "it's nae any o' your business ner mine."

"It'll be bad business for all of us if Dan Reinhardt doesn't kill Horne with the first shot."

Heather squinched up her face, but she said nothing as she set out a pudding she had made while Faron was at the meeting. Steam coils rose from the bubbling depths. She set two bowls and pewter spoons on the table, stood there waiting for her husband to sit down.

Faron sighed and took his pipe from his mouth. The pipestem was bitten nearly in two where his teeth had ground into the soft wood. He threw the pipe into the fireplace, watched the flames lap at it, devour it.

"That was your favorite pipe," said Heather.

"It's spoiled now," he said. "Evrathin' is spoiled."

Heather closed her eyes and said a silent prayer. Her husband was right, she knew. Faron was always right about men. She wondered now if there would ever be peace in Sky Valley. They had a government now, but they had vermin underfoot, as well, and not a pied-piper among the lot.

·CHAPTER 19·

HORNE AND MARY LEE MADE CAMP FOR TWO DAYS at Boiling Springs. He soaked in the healing waters as the newly-emerged sun burned off the snow, glinted off Pike's Peak and the smoky gray crags of the surrounding peaks that were etched in white, would be until high summer. No traveler marred their brief sojourn, no Ute passed, no scouting Mexican from Garcia's band.

"You know this country," said Mary Lee on the morning they left.

"Used to hunt South Park, traded with the Bents at their fort on the Arkansas."

"South Park. Is that the place east of here?"

"Yes. It is a good place."

"I never knew what it was called, but Red Hawk hunted there, too."

"I know," he replied, remembering.

* * *

He had been at Fort Laramie, drinking hard to forget the death of Malcolm, when he ran into Robert Fisher, an Indian trader for Bent, St. Vrain and Co. Fisher had told him about Bent's Fort, told him about the road there.

"You stay here and live in the past like the rest of these ex–mountain men, Horne, you'll be an old man by the time you're thirty. Learn the Injun trade. See some flat country. Fur tradin's over with. Forever."

"I know it," said Horne. It had been a year since the last rendezvous on the Green. Captain Andrew Drips had taken the caravan out of Westport, along with Bridger and Henry Fraeb, the last to leave the States, and there had been nothing but dream-talk and lies since at every trading post Horne had visited, worn out his welcome.

He had taken the road south from Fort Laramie along the foot of the mountains, passing near the old Indian camping grounds, to the South Platte River. He passed four Indian trading posts within twenty miles of one another, adobe blocks made into squares. Two of them, Fort Vasquez, once owned by Vasquez and Sublette, and Fort Lancaster, run by a little martinet named Lupton, an ex-army officer, were struggling to stay alive in heavy competition. Only Fort George, owned by the Bent, St. Vrain and Co. outfit, was doing any business. Sarpy and Fraeb's Fort Jackson was abandoned, falling to pieces, empty as the inside of a drum.

He had stayed at Little Raven's Arapaho village at the mouth of Cherry Creek, ate boiled puppy dog cooked in his honor. He was still Gray Wolf, then, and the Arapaho knew him as a brother to Red Hawk.

He remembered that trip as if it was yesterday, although he had made it more than a dozen years before, running from the memories of Malcolm, running from himself as fast as he could ride.

"That there's Jimmy's Camp Creek," he told Mary Lee, when they came to the stream that flowed into Fountain Creek.

"Why do they call it that?" she asked.

"Jimmy's Camp is east of here, a pretty little valley, ringed with a half-moon of pine-covered bluffs where there's a never-quit spring. Jimmy Daugherty was a trapper, come down from Laramie not long before I left the fort. He come to that spring and made camp. He was murdered there by his Mexican *compañero*. So, they called it Jimmy's Camp and maybe still do."

They crossed the creek and came to the juncture of the Fountain Creek.

"I know this creek," said Mary Lee. "It looks different in winter."

"The French called it the 'fountain that boils.' *La fontaine qui bouille*. Up above there's two mineral springs like the ones we saw. We got forty mile to go before we come to Gantt's."

"Is that where we're going?"

"It's near where Garcia's holed up, close to the Pueblo. I heard folks was living there. Gantt built him a good fort, better than most. I reckon the settlers took it over. I'll see if someone will take you in, while I go after Garcia."

Mary Lee shuddered. Horne kicked Tony's flanks, sent him surging ahead of her. This was not the time to talk about it. Horne's mind was made up. He was just trying to protect her, she knew, but she didn't want him to leave her. Not if he was.... She couldn't think about it. About Horne's getting killed. But the thought was there and it wouldn't go away. She looked at his strong back and felt a pang of want, a twisting need in the center of her belly. She wanted him at that moment worse than she had ever wanted him before.

Gantt's Fort lay six miles east of the Fountain and its junction with the Arkansas River. The adobe structure was built by John Gantt, an ex–army officer cashiered in '29 for falsifying his company's pay records. He took up trapping, and with his partner, Jefferson Blackwell, they camped on the Arkansas in '32. Near the mouth of the Purgatory he set his men to building winter quarters, log houses enclosed by a stockade. He traded with the Cheyenne and Arapaho for buffalo robes, was credited with setting up the whiskey trade along the Arkansas. He used a simple technique to accomplish this. John Gantt laced his firewater with sugar, called it "sweet medicine." The once-dry Indians couldn't get enough of it. Later, Gantt built his adobe fort, probably the first in the territory, and it was still standing when Horne and Mary Lee rode up to it on a mild spring-like day early in April.

Unlike the other settlements, Gantt's Fort had no wooden houses. Those who had built them at the other settlements had learned soon enough that the Indians loved to burn them down. Here at Gantt's, the settlers were wary and they were all armed. They opened the gate, waved the two riders inside.

"You see any Utes?" a man asked Horne.

"No."

"We got whiskey if you're dry, and Lupita Chacon will cook you dinner if'n you ast her."

"Thanks. I'm looking for information," said Horne, dismounting.

"We got old news, bad news, and no news. Suit yourself, stranger."

"The name's Horne."

"Jackson Horne? I'm Stanton Crawshaw and I driv up from Taos with Leegum a week ago."

"Barney Leegum?" asked Horne.

"The same. We lost our cattle to the Utes two weeks ago, and he's in that room over yonder where they pour whiskey. Damned Injuns been thicker'n ticks in summertime here lately."

Horne looked in the direction the man was pointing, saw a man sitting on a bench outside one of the dwellings nursing a bottle of Old Loudmouth or Taos Lightning. To Horne it was all the same, bad medicine for white man or red.

"I'll speak to Barney," said Horne. "You got a place where my woman can stay?"

"See Lupita. She has room, I reckon. That place in the corner."

The adobe fort was ringed with rooms around the square. There was an old fur-press in the center that had rusted over the years, a well, wooden benches outside the rooms. Men stood on the battlements armed with rifles, or sat just below the walls, talking quietly among themselves. The atmosphere was gloomy as Horne tied up Tony, shook the lead rope loose and led Gideon to a hitchrail on the opposite side of the plaza.

"Mary Lee," said Horne, "you talk to this Lupita Chacon, see if she won't put you up."

"I will," she said quietly, swinging down from her pony. She tried not to pout, but her face looked like a gray storm cloud as Horne stalked across the arena toward the cantina, his Spanish pistols on his belt, the Colt Navy tucked in next to his knife. He carried the Hawken in his hand. His shadow shrank beneath him in the center of the square, fell behind him in a ragged puddle as he crossed to the other side.

The man on the bench sat up straight, looked bleary-eyed at Horne.

"Where ya goin', pilgrim? Bar huntin'?"

"I was lookin' for a jackass," said Horne.

"I don't see none hereabouts."

"That's funny," retorted Horne, "I see one right now."

The man snorted, slapped his knee. He held up the bottle to Horne.

"You got me on that one, stranger. Have a pull."

"Thanks," said Horne. "Save me a swallow. I got business with Leegum."

"That white-eyed sonofabitch, go on ahead. He wouldn't give you the sweat off his balls."

Horne walked into the cantina, squinted at the shift of light. It was dark, gloomy, with only the pale sunlight filtering through the door and a trapdoor in the ceiling to give it illumination. The single room was filled with hard-eyed men and settlers with the look of fear in their eyes—as if they had been pushed into a corner and expected at any moment to be scalped or slain or disemboweled by an unseen enemy.

"Well, I'll be a hornswoggled sonofabitch," said a man at the far end of what served as a bar. Someone had nailed two by tens or twelves to barrels, set them in high mounds of dirt, and slicked the whipsawed boards down with sandstone and oil.

"Barney," said Horne.

"Horne, thet ain't you," said Leegum, a chunky man with a lumpy, beestung face and a milk-eye that wandered like an eight-ball in its socket while the other eye, hazel-brown, sometimes green, remained fixed as painted glass ninety percent of the time. "Some Mexes come here and said you was dead."

"They try to sell you any horses?"

"Yar, they did."

"Garcia?"

"He was one of 'em."

"You buy any?"

"Nope. Nobody in his bunch could produce a legible bill of sale."

"That's because he stole 'em," said Horne.

"I figgered. Your'n?"

Horne nodded. "I want 'em back," he said. "Need to hire a few men to help me get 'em, drive 'em up to LaPorte."

"I opine that might be easier said than done," said Leegum. "Nobody hereabouts like Pedro Garcia much, but nobody wants to buck up against him, neither."

"Three men. Top dollar."

"Have a drink, Horne."

"I'm in a hurry, Barney. Any of you men want to ride with me?"

The others turned away and the sour smell of fear soaked the air in the room.

"Pedro cuts a wide swath in this part of the country," said Leegum. "Him and thet pard of his, Delgado."

Horne looked at a man a few feet away.

"How about you?" Horne asked him.

"Mister, they ain't nobody in this room wants to hire out to you. Pedro can put together a dozen greasers at any one time and never bat an eye."

"I'll pay good money," persisted Horne.

"It ain't a question of money," said the man. "It's a question of how bad a man wants to stay alive. Twixt the Mexes and the Utes this bunch is pretty spooked and I'm among 'em. We got famblys."

"That it, Leegum?" Horne swung his gaze to Barney.

"You heard him right, Horne. Garcia and his bunch have holed up back of the Pueblo like a swarm of hornets. You go in there after him and you ain't comin' back."

Horne swept the room with a raking gaze and turned on his heel.

"Buy you a drink—anytime," called out Lee-gum. Horne said nothing.

Mary Lee was talking to a Mexican woman. They both looked up when Horne entered the room.

"I'm goin', Mary Lee," he said.

"You hire on some men to help you?"

Horne shook his head.

"You—you can't go after Garcia alone."

"I'll be back," he said, touching the brim of his hat. He walked across the square, shoved the Hawken in its boot and climbed into the saddle.

"Open the gate," he called out. The men in the cantina came outside to watch him ride out.

"So long, Horne," said Leegum. "Right nice to see you again."

The gate swung open and Horne rode through without a word.

There wasn't a man there who thought that he would ever be back.

• CHAPTER 20 •

HORNE KEPT TO THE ARROYOS AND THE DRY CREEK beds, south of the river. He rode up on the deserted Pueblo, circled it, looking at the empty bastions, the pickets atop the walls, the open gates, the mounds of graves outside. He rode slow, listening, headed for the hills to the west. Sometimes he took the high ground for a look.

He heard the horses long before he saw them. He patted Tony's neck to keep him quiet. When he saw the Mexican riders, he slipped off Tony's back, pulled the Hawken from its boot. His possibles pouch dangled under his left arm, heavy with powder and ball. He ground-tied the horse and went toward the riders on foot, cougar-quiet, a plan in his mind that emerged out of a conversation he'd had with Mary Lee only days before. As he looked at the terrain ahead he wondered if one man might not be able to overcome many with a

165

simple trick that he remembered from his boy-hood.

"Horne, you can't go up against Garcia and his men without help," she had said.

"I'll see if I can find some men to help me," he said.

"And what if you can't?"

"I don't know. I was thinkin' about when I was a boy, back in Kentucky. Used to hunt turkeys all by myself."

Mary Lee snorted.

"I'd make the calls with my mouth. Pretty good at it, too. I'd bring those hens and gobblers up to the ridge. Sometimes they'd all be walking single-file along the top of a holler. I'd pick 'em off one by one with my forty caliber flintlock. It was a fine little rifle, Kentucky-made by a German smith."

"Didn't your shots scare the birds?" Mary Lee asked.

"I'd take the bird in the rear of the line and gobble after each shot. The birds in front never looked back. Just ahead where I was a-gobblin'. Once, I hit a young Tom and he flapped and the old Tom came up and attacked him. I got both birds."

"What're you thinkin', Horne?"

"Well, I could draw some of them Mexes out, maybe pick them off until the odds are more even."

"That's crazy. Mexicans aren't turkeys."

"No, I reckon that's so. But I got an idea."

"What's that?"

"I'll let you know if it works," he had said with a grin.

He came up on the first Mexican quiet. The Mexican drew his rifle from his scabbard. Horne shot him out of the saddle with one of the pistols. The second man rode up, rifle blazing. Horne shot him, too. The shots aroused the others and Horne heard them shouting in Spanish. He backed off, lay behind a little knoll, reloaded his two pistols.

One by one, the Mexicans rode out to find the shooter, and Horne picked them off—three, in all—and they never saw him. He shifted his position, reloaded quickly. He circled the camp and the corrals. He recognized his horses. When the Mexicans were all strung out, hunting him, he picked them off, one by one. He kept moving, always moving, and they couldn't find him in the scrub brush. He reloaded and picked his shots.

Garcia yelled hoarsely. "*Mátalo. Mata a aquel gringo cabrón.*"

"Garcia," called Horne. "Turn out my horses and clear out, or I'll make wolfmeat out of you."

"Horne, *tú cabrón de la chingada.*"

Horne sent a fifty caliber ball sizzling past Garcia's ear.

"*Cuidado,*" husked Luis Delgado.

"*Abre la puerta,*" growled Garcia. Horne reloaded, saw them plain. He was invisible in the clumps of sagebrush, and he kept moving, hunched low. He made no sound. Delgado opened the corral gates, and the horses streamed out, headed for open country to the east, toward Pueblo.

"Horne, *voy a matarte pronto, me entiendes?*" yelled Garcia.

"Pedro, if I ever see your ugly face again, I'll blow you to hell."

Horne caught up Tony, mounted him. He lay low atop his horse as he caught up with the runaway herd, but no man followed him. He brought the horses under control, settled them down. They raised a cloud of reddish dust in the air. He drove them into the stables at Gantt's Fort, and the

Americans watched him ride in, bark orders to the stableman. The stableman opened up a corral and Horne ran them in expertly.

"Buy you a drink, Horne," said Barney Leegum, tipping his hat back off his forehead.

Horne looked at him with narrowed eyes.

"I'll need to hire a hand or two to help me take these horses back to LaPorte."

"There's a man or two who'd go."

"I'll have a drink with you, then."

Pedro Garcia roared with anger. Two of his men were stone dead, five others were shot up. Luis Delgado patched them up, but he soon joined Pedro and helped him put away the tequila.

"We should have killed him," said Garcia. "These men are stupid."

"This Horne, he is some man," said Delgado. "He does not do what you expect him to do."

"He is a bastard," said Garcia. The two men spoke in Spanish. "I should have killed him a long time ago."

"Yes, that is true. Maybe you will kill him one day."

"I will kill him."

"When? How?"

"I will wait until he has dropped off the horses and gone back home. I will ride back up there to that valley above the Poudre and kill him."

"Yes, that would be a good place. In summer, maybe, when the weather is good."

"Yes. Late summer, before the leaves have turned."

And Garcia thought about it as he drank the clear liquid fire. It was April now, and it would take Horne some time to take his horses up to the high country for the summer. When he was most busy, Pedro would go there and shoot him. Then, it would be over and he could forget about the woman Horne had stolen from him, about the humiliation of those years since Santa Fe. The bastard. Pedro would be more careful next time. Next time, he would kill Horne and everyone would know that he was the better man. This was a matter of honor with Pedro Garcia. Manhood was everything. *Machismo*.

Horne hired two hands, Brad Meadows and Jerald Wakefield, to help him drive the horses back to LaPorte. Brad was a bearded, wiry young man from Missouri, with pale blue eyes and a quiet manner. Wakefield was broad of chest and shoulder, a hunter skillful with either rifle or bow, since he had lived among the Indians of the northern plains. He looked Nordic, with his blond hair and steely blue eyes sunk behind high cheekbones, but he was of English stock, he told Horne, with "maybe a little Irish thrown in fer meanness." Along the way, Jerald told Horne that his woman was sick.

"She ain't my woman," Horne snapped at him, but he noticed that Mary Lee would go off by herself every morning and get sick.

"How long's this been going on?" he asked her.

"Since—since we left Sky Valley."

He looked at her belly, saw the slight swelling. He hadn't noticed it before. Mary Lee bowed her head, avoided looking at him for a long moment.

"It ain't mine," he said.

She broke into tears, looked at him defiantly. "Well, no one said it was yours. It's mine. Now, leave me alone and mind your own business."

Horne began to walk on eggshells around her. He took pains to shorten the day. He picked out the easiest paths to follow and he became solicitous of her feelings. Horne began to change from a self-confident, strapping six-foot-three brute into an awkward schoolboy.

It didn't dawn on him until later that the child Mary Lee was carrying must have been fathered by Red Hawk. One day when they were alone, he brought up the subject.

"You ain't goin' to keep it, are you?"

"What?" she exclaimed, horrified.

"That pup you carry in your belly."

"Horne, what's the matter with you?"

"That's Red Hawk's whelp, ain't it?" He felt as if he'd stepped square on a hornet's nest. Horne felt very uncomfortable, but he was going to bull his way through the conversation, come hell or high water.

"That's none of your damned business, Horne."

"You give birth to a breed under my roof, it's my business. A bastard at that."

"I was hoping you'd become the child's father."

"Me? Woman, your folks don't like me as it is. You pop with a half-breed, an Arapaho to boot, and everyone in that valley will come after me with pitch and chicken feathers."

Mary Lee laughed. Horne felt his anger rise unbidden. He clenched his fists, spluttered to defend himself. Before he could say any more, Mary Lee rode off, proud and swollen, holding her head up high.

They dropped the horses off in LaPorte and Horne told Dave to sell the best to the army, keep Champ and Coal. Sheppers had some bad news for Horne. He told him while Horne was feeding some of the yearling foals Dave had brought over from the other ranch. The foals belonged to Sheppers. Mary Lee watched as he played with them, rubbed them affectionately.

"That man Reinhardt was down a couple of

weeks ago," Sheppers told Horne. "Wearing a tin star. Says he's the sheriff of Sky Valley."

"So, they got 'em a town."

"He said you was wanted for murder."

"Who am I supposed to have killed?"

"That Frenchie, Moreaux, and his woman."

Horne stood up. The foals jumped at his sudden movement, pranced away.

"Jules is dead? Maria?"

"That's what the man said."

Horne swore.

"Maybe you'd better not go back up there," said Dave.

"No. It's my home," said Horne.

"You can't fight the law, right or wrong, Jack."

"Their law ain't my law."

"Horne," Mary Lee said later, "you have a gentleness in you. The way you treated those foals. I can't understand how you can kill a man like you killed Red Hawk, Newcastle, and not have any feelings about it."

"I got feelings about it," he gruffed, but he stalked away without explanation. He was thinking about Jules Moreaux and wondering who had killed him and his wife.

Sheppers made several oblique references to Mary Lee's condition while they were there until Horne reared back and flared up with anger, told him to shut up. He knew, then, it was time to go up the mountain. On the ride back up the Poudre, Mary Lee was very uncomfortable. She was very near her time, Horne knew. Shortly after they arrived back at his cabin, Mary Lee went into labor. No one had seen them. No one knew they were back yet.

There was nothing for Horne to do but help de-

171

liver the baby. Mary Lee, sweating, her face contorted in pain, grunted and cried out.

"Take it," she screamed. "Horne, take the baby."

Awkwardly, he reached down, some instinct telling him that he had to pull the child from the womb. He saw only a wet, matted mass of hair, the outline of a tiny head. He stood there helplessly, afraid to touch any part of her, the baby.

"Damn you, Horne," she gasped, "pull it free. It's coming now, I can feel it."

The head popped through the opening and tiny shoulders slick with blood and fluids oozed out. He grasped them gently in his big hands and pulled as Mary Lee bore down with her hips. It came, then, the child, squint-faced and ugly, streaked red with blood, coated with sticky matter. Its umbilical, like a twisted sausage, held the child to its mother's womb. Horne turned the newborn over on its back, drew his knife and cut the cord, freeing the tiny life from its former blood and food supply.

Mary Lee sighed deeply and smiled.

Horne saw that the child was a boy. It looked like an oversized rat and it made no sound, but worked its hands into fists, opened and closed them as if it was dying. He jiggled it and the infant's lungs filled. The child squawled and kicked in his hands.

He looked at Mary Lee with wonder. He didn't understand the miracle fully, but he knew that something marvelous had happened, that this child had lived in a dark sea for months, hidden from the world. Something tugged hard deep inside him, something long-ago forgotten, something long buried, and he thought of life and that tenuous thread that bound all creatures in the universe and he was humbled by the enormity of it, by the awesome secret that made it possible for a woman to create life in her belly.

"Give him to me, Horne. Give me the baby."

Horne handed the infant to her and she nestled it in her arms, smiled down at the creature with its eyes clenched tightly shut and its toothless mouth sucking in air that it had never tasted until now. He turned away, sodden with sweat, overpowered by the miracle he had just witnessed.

Mary Lee was very happy. "I'm going to call him Jackson Hawk," she told Horne.

Horne scowled and swore hard for ten seconds.

"Ought to take the little bastard and dash its head against a tree," he muttered.

Gary Winder rode by one day, saw Mary Lee outside, holding the infant, cooing and coddling it in her arms. He rode home and told his father, Chollie, who sent word to Lou Simmons. The major was infuriated. Elizabeth Simmons goaded her husband into going to see Horne to ask if he had married their daughter. "But don't do it angry, Lou. Just see what you can see. Ask if Mary Lee needs us. Maybe she wants to come back home."

"I'll not have a bastard child in my home," said Lou.

Elizabeth put her arms around her husband, began to sob. "Oh, can't you let out the love that's in you?" she pleaded. "Think of Mary Lee, instead of yourself."

"Oh, leave me be, woman," he said, and stormed out of the cabin.

Lou borrowed a horse from Bill McPherson, rode over to Horne's cabin. Horne met him outside and Lou asked him the question that he'd practiced all morning.

"No, we're not married," said Horne.

"By god, you'll pay for this," said Simmons.

Mary Lee stepped out of the cabin.

"Pa," she said, "don't you want to see your grandson?"

"No, by damned. I have no grandson."

"Just look at him, Pa. He has your eyes, Ma's nose."

Her father glared at her and turned the horse, rode away.

"Pa, please," she shouted, but there was no answer. She crumpled, then, and Horne took her in his arms. She sobbed hysterically, beat her small fists against Horne's chest.

Horne took her inside, spoke soothingly to her, and began playing with the baby.

"He'll come around," he told her. "He's just riled some with me. Don't fret about it."

"Oh, Horne, what do you know? He hates me. He hates the baby. So do you."

"No," he said softly. "No I don't no more."

Simmons did not return home. He rode to Reinhardt's place, the anger still burning hot in his vitals. Maybe he would take her back if Horne was out of the way. Maybe he could change her back to the way she was.

"Horne's back," he said. "I want you to kill him. The sonofabitch has sired a bastard with my daughter. I want him dead. I'll pay good money. Once he's out of the way, I'll have my daughter back."

"What about the kid, Simmons?"

"I'll deal with that problem later."

"I'll see what I can do," said Reinhardt, grinning.

• CHAPTER 21 •

THE SUMMER WANED AND AUTUMN COLORS RE-
placed the green. The aspen leaves turned
golden yellow and the elk began to bugle in
the high meadows. Horne knew he must make a
trip to LaPorte to check on his horses, bring back
winter supplies.

"I'll be back before the snow flies," he told Mary
Lee.

"I'll be waiting," she said, holding little Jack in
her arms. Her face glowed and Horne knew she
was truly happy. He liked the little tyke and Mary
Lee was a good mother. He shook his head and
waved goodbye. Tony stepped out quickly,
proudly.

Some distance down the Poudre, Horne cut the
tracks of three horses. He read them, saw that the
men had spotted him and then turned off the trail
as if to hide. This thought bothered him all the
way to LaPorte.

* * *

Garcia, Berthoud and Delgado rode up to Mc-Gonigle's, a few hours later. They tied their horses at the hitchrail, went inside to buy whiskey. Reinhardt was there, took the three men aside.

"You up here after Horne?" asked Reinhardt.

"We have come to kill him," said Garcia.

"Good," said Reinhardt. "I been thinkin' the same thing myself. I'll help you."

"Got to wait until he gets back," said Delgado.

"Huh?"

"Horne is riding down the Poudre," said Jacques Berthoud. "I am sure it was him."

"Why didn't you kill him, then?" asked Reinhardt.

"We were not sure, and it was not a good place," said Delgado.

Lou Simmons came into McGonigle's and sat at the table with the three men. He nodded to Berthoud.

"They're here to take care of Horne for you, Simmons," Reinhardt said. "Only Horne ain't here."

"He'll be back," said Simmons. "He always rides down to the flat this time of year to bring in his winter supplies. You going to wait for him?"

"We will wait for him," said Garcia, pulling on the whiskey bottle. "I am going to kill Horne myself."

Simmons smiled, slapped Reinhardt on the back. "Now, I can get my daughter back, bastard or no bastard."

"What?" asked Garcia.

"Horne sullied my daughter," said Lou. "She's got his kid."

Garcia looked at Delgado, a strange smile on his face. Simmons missed it, but not Reinhardt or

Berthoud. Jacques shivered, poured himself a stiff drink from the whiskey bottle.

"So, what is this kid?" asked Garcia.

"A boy," said Simmons. "You bring me Horne's scalp and I'll pay you a hundred dollars apiece."

"That is good," said Garcia. "We will ride after Horne very soon."

Later, Reinhardt watched the three men mount their horses.

"You really going after Horne?"

"No," said Garcia. "We will first kill the thing Horne loves most."

"The kid?"

"And his woman," leered Delgado.

"Then we will wait for Horne's return," said Garcia. "He won't be long. We stopped by the Sheppers place and watered our horses. He will tell Horne that we are looking for him, I think."

"Pedro, you are one smart *hombre*," said Reinhardt.

"I am plenty smart," agreed Garcia.

When Horne learned from Dave Sheppers that Garcia, Delgado, and Berthoud had ridden through LaPorte, headed up the Poudre, he put two and two together and left a list of supplies for Dave to fill and bring up.

"I'm going back to Sky Valley."

"I'll take care of it," said Dave.

Horne rode away, spurring Tony into a run toward the trail where the Poudre leaves the mountains. A terrible sense of dread darkened his thoughts, made him push Tony. He had felt the same way when about to leave Perla that time. Garcia would not have killed her if he had taken her away. Now, he felt the same urgency. He raced up the Poudre, hoping that what he feared most would not happen. But he knew the heart of Garcia, knew that he would stop at nothing to hurt Horne.

Garcia, Berthoud and Delgado hid near Horne's cabin and waited.

"Do you have the coal oil, Luis?" asked Garcia.

"Yes, and *fósforos*, the matches."

Berthoud opened his mouth to protest, but said nothing. His throat was dry and he was woozy from the alcohol. But he didn't like any of this. He didn't like it at all. He shivered in the late afternoon sun.

From their vantage point they would be able to see Horne when he returned. It might be two days, or three or four, but they wanted to be ready. They had made camp up in the trees and they could watch the cabin from a wide shelf that was hidden by spruce and pine.

"I want him to see his woman and child, first," whispered Garcia. "Then, we will burn them out. I will kill her, the baby, and then him."

"That is good," grinned Delgado. He held up a sulphur match, struck it with his thumbnail. The blaze flared up, lit his cruel features for a brief moment.

Horne rode up to his cabin the next day, his senses fully alert. Tony was well-lathered from the hard ride. Horne stripped him quickly, put him in the corral without rubbing him down. There was a terrible silence about the place, and his dread turned to cold fear.

"Mary Lee," he called. But there was no answer. He stepped up to the cabin door, cocked the Hawken in his hand. "Mary Lee, let me in."

The door opened a moment later. Mary Lee stood there, her face waxen. She clutched the baby to her bosom. Horne saw that she was trembling.

"What's the matter?" he asked.

"Horne, I'm so glad to see you. I'm frightened out of my wits."

"Why? Who was here?"

"Those Mexicans are out there," she whimpered. "I saw them when I went to feed my pony. They're up on that outcropping where the spruce are thick. I think I saw Jacques Berthoud there, too. I know why they've come. They're going to kill us all."

"God, Mary Lee," he said, "I'm sorry."

"What are we going to do?"

"You hide in here. I'll go out and try to circle around them."

"Horne, I—I'm afraid."

He took her and the baby in his arms. He kissed her on the cheek.

"Quick, you get hid and stay put. No matter what happens, don't come outside."

"Horne is back," said Berthoud. "That's his horse down there."

Garcia and Delgado peered over the edge of the shelf.

"Mount up," ordered Garcia.

Moments later, atop their horses, they saw Horne come out, Hawken in hand.

"You stay here, Pancho," Garcia told Berthoud. "Cover us. Luis, you give me the coal oil and have your *fósforos* ready." The two Mexicans charged, firing at Horne. Horne ducked back inside the cabin. Garcia splashed coal oil on the logs as they rode in a tight circle around the cabin. Delgado struck a sulphur match and tossed it into a pool of coal oil. The cabin caught fire, sending billows of smoke into the sky.

Garcia called out to Horne.

"How do you like it now, *cabrón*?"

Horne dashed outside, pushing Mary Lee and the baby in front of him. "Into the barn," he said. "Take this," he said, handing her the Hawken, "and hide."

He scrambled for cover as shots boomed out. Garcia cursed, rode into the woods, Delgado right behind him. He frantically reloaded, as Horne drew both his pistols and raced toward the two Mexicans. Delgado fired his pistol, missed. Horne ran a zig-zag pattern as Garcia rammed the ball home in his rifle. Horne shot him in the gut. The Mexican doubled over in pain. Delgado spurred his horse up the slope. Horne fired at him, saw him twitch, but he stayed in the saddle. He kicked Garcia's weapon away, stood over him.

"How did you find me?" he asked.

"Easy," croaked Garcia. "The people here do not like you much. Simmons and Reinhardt have much hate for you, *gringo*. Jaeger, too. But we were here before. Luis, he killed that Frenchman and Reinhardt killed his wife."

Horne reloaded his pistols. Taking careful aim, he fired at Garcia from close range. The ball fractured the frontplate of the Mexican's skull, blew his brains out the back.

He started up the hill after Delgado, reloading from his possibles pouch, his dread deepening with every labored step.

Jacques Berthoud crept into the small log barn.

"Miss Simmons," he called. "Come, I'll help you. You must get away."

Mary Lee trembled in fear. Strong arms held her in a steely grip. A hand clamped her mouth tightly shut.

"Miss Simmons? It is Jacques. I come to help you. Delgado . . ."

Jacques froze as Delgado stepped out from one

of the stalls, Mary Lee Simmons in his grasp. He held a knife in his hand. In horror, Berthoud watched as Luis shoved the knife into Mary Lee's throat, jerked the blade upward, then outward. A fountain of blood gushed from the wound. The baby dropped from her arms and she pitched forward, a look of ghastly terror in her fading eyes.

Berthoud brought his rifle up, but he was too late. Delgado threw the knife, hurled it fullforce at Jacques's chest. It struck the Frenchman near the heart and he staggered backwards. Delgado drew his pistol, fired it pointblank at the wounded man. White smoke filled the barn, obscured Delgado's view as Jacques fell into a slump against the tackroom door.

Luis struck a match, dropped it next to Mary Lee's body. Smoke coiled in the straw, began to flutter as the flame burrowed deep. He stepped out the back door as the flame exploded in the dry barn, sent a lashing tongue of flame down its length.

Horne was waiting for him, both pistols cocked.

"Is my woman in there?" he asked.

"Sure, *gringo*, what you think? Too bad I didn't have time to show her what a real man was like."

Horne squeezed both triggers. Delgado's face disappeared in a cloud of blood. Horne leaped over him as his body struck the ground. He fought through the smoke, but the flames drove him back. He ran around to the front. Berthoud's body lay beneath the pall of thick smoke where he had crawled after being shot. He was dead, and the flames made his skin crackle and pop as they swarmed over his waist, feeding hungrily on his flesh.

"Mary Lee!" Horne screamed as he held up his arms to shield his face from the heat.

There was no answer, but he swore he heard the

baby scream once before the roar of the fire drowned out all but the sound of Horne's own sobbing.

The people from the town saw the billows of smoke rising in the air from Horne's place.

"What you figger?" Jaeger asked his brother-in-law, Reinhardt.

"It looks like Horne's goin' up in smoke. Reckon them Mexes burned him out?"

"I don't like it none. Horne might be back, blame us."

"I would worry," advised Faron MacGregor, "if I were you. You could ride out over Cameron Pass and he might not catch you for a week or so."

Reinhardt paled, but jutted his chin out. "I'm not afraid of Horne."

"Me, neither," said Jaeger.

"Suit yoursel'," said MacGregor.

Elizabeth Simmons called over to her husband. "Louis, I'm worried about Mary Lee. You go find out what's happening."

"I'm not goin' by myself," said Lou. "Anyone want to ride over there with me?"

No one answered him.

Horne rode up, pulling the two Mexican horses. Delgado and Garcia were draped over the high-cantled saddles, toes down. He cut the lashings, dumped them in front of McGonigle's, looked at the men lined up on the porch. Reinhardt, Jaeger, Simmons. Behind them, MacGregor, McPherson, and the Winders waited in silence, watching.

"What you doin' that for?" asked a belligerent Jaeger. "This ain't no garbage pile."

"Maybe it is," said Horne, and they all noticed the Hawken across the pommel, the brace of Spanish pistols hooked onto his belt.

"Well, it's your mess," said Reinhardt imperiously. "That ain't none of our doin'."

"I think it is your doin'," said Horne. "You sicked those dogs on me and I brung 'em back. Simmons, you poor miserable sonofabitch, they killed your daughter and grandson."

Lou Simmons cried out and Elizabeth came running from their cabin, her skirt flapping at her ankles.

"Is it true?" she wailed.

"Yes, ma'am. Jacques Berthoud tried to stop it, I reckon, but Delgado killed him. They're the ones who killed Jules Moreaux and his woman, too. Garcia named Reinhardt and said Jaeger was in on it."

The men on the porch shifted the weight on their feet, dropped their heads for a long moment. One or two shot murderous looks at Reinhardt.

"So sad," said MacGregor. "Such a pretty girl she was and such a terrible shame. And Jules and his lovely wife. A curse on you, Reinhardt."

The others nodded in assent before Elizabeth commanded their attention.

"What's burning?" she screamed.

"Everything I own," said Horne. "Everything I had. Everything. I couldn't get 'em out, Mrs. Simmons." He choked on the words, strangled with the grief that gripped him, tore at his senses, shuddered through him like an angry wind.

Elizabeth looked at Horne's smoke-blackened face and screamed again before fainting.

Chollie beckoned to his son, Gary. "Fetch your mother and some of the other women," he said softly. "Hurry."

"Horne," said McPherson, "seems to me you got your satisfaction with those two Mexicans. You're not welcome here in the settlement. Wherever you go, there is blood and death."

"So, you're in with Reinhardt and Simmons," said Horne.

"We want a decent town here. What's done is done. We'll punish our own, lay blame where blame belongs."

"You call this decent? You send mad dogs to murder a defenseless woman and her child?"

"You never should have taken up with Mary Lee," muttered McPherson.

"That's none of your business," said Horne.

"Lou wasn't right in his head. He had good reason to hate you, Horne. The Lord will see to his punishment as he will see to yours."

Horne looked at them all coldly.

"Reinhardt," he said, "you and Jaeger there have got an hour to clear out of this valley. If you don't go, you'll die here."

"We don't want killers here, either," said Mc-Pherson.

"Those two are just as much murderers as the Mexicans were," said Horne. "I can't prove Reinhardt was in on any of this, but Garcia had nothing to lose when he told me about killing Moreaux and his wife. Garcia said as much about Jaeger there, whoever the hell he is. Not a damned one of you knows what settling means. I came here in peace and I mean to stay here in peace if I can. You don't build a town by picking and choosing who's to live in it. People make a town by learning how to live peaceable with one another."

"The mon's right," said MacGregor.

Chollie Winder was silent. He was staring at Reinhardt's and Jaeger's backs. His hand rested on a pistol tucked in his belt.

"You two get packing," Horne said, gesturing with the Hawken.

Reinhardt made a move toward his pistol. Chollie drew his and rammed the muzzle into Reinhardt's back. Jaeger froze.

"I think maybe you had better do what Mr. Horne says," urged Chollie.

Sheepishly, the two men left the porch. They mounted their horses and rode off on the trail through the valley.

"If I find any man on my trapline, I'll shoot him dead," Horne told the others. "And, I'd think real hard and twice more about coming to my side of this valley. I've got some rebuilding to do before the snow flies. I filed on a hundred and sixty acres some time back and I'll blaze my boundaries so you know where you ain't wanted."

"By what law do you order those men out of the valley, and kill those who get in your way?" asked McPherson.

"By my law," said Horne, hefting his rifle. He touched his heels to Tony's flanks, swung the horse in a tight turn.

"There's a man with the bark still on him," observed Chollie Winder. "I hope those boys don't try to jump Horne."

Moments later, like an answer to a prophecy, they heard the rattle of firing, then it was still.

"I knew they wouldn't leave peaceable," said Chollie Winder. "Damn fools."

"Maybe we're the fools," said MacGregor. "I wonder if this valley is big enough for any of us and a man like Horne."

"Maybe not," said McPherson, with a deep sigh. "A man like that needs a lot of room."

"Aye," said MacGregor.

Two riderless horses loped up to McGonigle's, reins trailing. They stopped and snorted, pawed the ground. Neither horse belonged to Horne.

Elizabeth and Lou looked up, still clutching each other in their sudden grief.

"Come on, boys," said McPherson. "Looks like we got some buryin' to do."

That night, a lone wolf found the graves the men had dug and sat atop them, howling mournfully. There wasn't a man in Sky Valley who did not feel the early chill in the solemn autumn air.